Trap!

No one was visible on the grounds as Diana moved away from the house. Her pace quickened as she moved into the shadow of the pines. The forbidding hulk of the Devereau family mausoleum reared in the edge of her vision, and she stopped, eye caught by a needle of reflected sunlight.

She left the path to investigate, and discovered the beacon: a pair of spectacles, one lens broken. Fine links of a neck chain shimmered in the sunlight . . . Cloty's glasses! Diana stared at the mausoleum. Was the missing Cloty there? A chill seeped out and seemed to envelop her as she forced herself to move toward the rusty gates. With a shock, she saw her hands tugging at the iron doors . . . then she was inside.

"Cloty?" The ragged word echoed faintly. She ventured another few steps . . . and then spun about, screaming, as the iron doors clanged shut . . .

Dark Over Acadia
Anne Talmage

MAGNUM  EDITIONS

MAGNUM BOOKS
NEW YORK

DARK OVER ACADIA

PRESTIGE BOOKS INC. • 18 EAST 41ST STREET
NEW YORK, N.Y. 10017

Chapter 1

Impatient with the final miles of heat-seared swampland still separating her from Devereau House, Diana Latham refused the urge to press the gas pedal of her dusty compact car another notch.

Alone, luggage piled in back, she was already driving as fast as she dared on the narrow, primitive road that writhed torturously through the muggy desolation of the Lousiana delta.

She shifted under the steering wheel to ease the twing of back muscles beginning to feel the wear of the long trip.

The road ahead wavered in a lake-like shimmering of heat, and Diana saw a yellow-splotched mass humped near the center line. The humming of the compact's little engine caused the mass to stir, to elongate itself, a huge snake sunning on the scorching heat of the black macadam.

With a gasp, flashing her toe to the brake, Diana

watched the evilly beautiful creature slither from sight in a tangle of sawgrass.

Resuming speed, she drew a shaky breath through a small, gamin smile. This certainly wasn't the place to get a wheel stuck in a ditch or have a flat tire.

But nothing could really dampen her eagerness for the first glimpse of Lucy Devereau's home and the sight of Lucy herself.

We'll gabble until all hours, Diana thought, catching up on everything that's happened in the year since we've seen each other . . .

Her thicker-than-blood friendship with Lucy had an unlikely beginning three years ago, when as Peace Corps volunteers they were assigned to the poverty-stricken village of Iaxtaca in the Peruvian Andes.

She'd wondered at first if Lucy would make the grade—or forward a request to be relieved when the rattling, coughing weekly bus next chugged laboriously into Iaxtaca.

Wholly feminine and slenderly lovely, Diana was by no means a Calamity Jane in buckskin. In comparison with the lot of the Iaxtacans, Diana had been well off. Nevertheless, she had known something of grief, loss, hardship. She went to Iaxtaca without illusions as to what she was getting into.

It was obvious that Lucy, on the other hand, came from a wealth-oozing background that provided all the pampering little shields, the insulation, against the barbs and ugliness of life.

Diana needn't have worried. Lucy had the quiet, gritty habit of somehow rising to the occasion, from grubbing in an old widow's garden patch to round-the-clock nursing of a dying child.

As their friendship developed, Lucy would sometimes reminisce about her plantation home in far-off Louisiana. From these spoken bits and pieces, Diana gradually built a mental image of Devereau House. Age-mellowed white colonial, with columned veranda. Tall chimneys at either end etching the swampland sky like towers guarding a gracious sanctuary. A house of heirlooms and memories. A house that—like the generations of its family—had survived pestilence, famine, floods, and wars.

At the moment of separation a year ago in San Francisco's International Airport, Diana and Lucy had faced each other. Filled with emotion, they were oblivious to the hustle about them.

Lucy's eyes had brimmed. "Well, I guess this is it, Diana. Me for home—and you on your way to a teaching job in Kansas. But you won't forget your promise next summer? A guest room at Devereau House will be waiting."

"I'll be there," Diana said, "bag and baggage, not later than the end of June. As soon as school is out, I'll have to spend a few days at Bankhead's Crossing in Kansas."

7

This, as Lucy knew, was the crossroads town near the farm where Diana's foster parents lived, a surly, penurious uncle and his thin, embittered wife. They had grudgingly taken Diana when she was five, after her natural parents had died within a week of each other. Once, she had come close to hating the couple; but now, in adulthood, she had long since put much of the old feelings aside. She owed the old couple a debt of respect; they had put a roof over her head; and they had, with some mutterings on the subject, doled out a pittance which, combined with a scholastic scholarship and part-time work, had enabled Diana to continue her education.

"I understand," Lucy had nodded. "But I wish you were coming tomorrow, Diana! There'll be parties and boys. Horses to ride. Creole dinners like you've never tasted. Trips down the delta to New Orleans. Devereau House was made for nice, long visits—and it will be the summer of a lifetime!"

The summer—here at last . . .

Diana slowed the humming compact as the road ahead split in a fork. She took the left turn, as the storekeeper in the village five miles behind had instructed when she stopped to inquire.

In the range of Diana's vision was a vast, lush, junglelike desolation. The limitless sky was a scorching blue mantel. For the past few hours,

Diana's surroundings had gradually changed as she drove deeper into the delta. Now it seemed that she had slipped by subtle degrees into a strange never-never land dotted with tiny clapboard villages, with here and there a weathered pine-frame shack built on stilts at the edge of a bayou.

This was Cajun country, and Diana recalled how Lucy had once described it: "A world of its own, where the native dialect is a mixture of French, Spanish, English. It's still more French-colonial than automated American. Fellow from the Indochina rice paddies could feel right at home there."

Diana glanced at the odometer. "When the left fork has been taken," the lanky, sallow store-keeper had said, "Devereau House turn-off is a hop and jump five miles past the front bumper."

Four miles yet to go. Diana's gaze swept the countryside. Sawgrass and palmetto stood with greasy green lifelessness in the heat. Tangled forests of mangrove and pine humped against the horizon. In the furthest westward distance a thin finger of smoke spiraled skyward. It marked perhaps a sawmill where lean, sun-leathered men were felling centuries-old cypress.

Diana gave her head a short shake, thinking of the pioneer Acadians who'd first come to this land. They were refugees, driven from northland homes when the British had wrested control of

Canada from the French more than two hundred years ago. The British had re-named the Acadian homeland, calling it Nova Scotia.

Diana wondered how the Acadians had picked such an unlikely, far-off destination. No one knew for certain. Louisiana was French at the time, and the back-delta country offered peace and a chance to build in a land no one else wanted. Not until later was the wealth in soil, furs, and oil revealed.

The miracle was that any had finished the trek at all, covering thousands of unmapped miles of wilderness filled with all the threats of nature and hostile Indians.

The first Devereau had been among that small group of survivors, building his pole-and-thatch cabin near the spot where a later generation would lay the foundations for Devereau House.

To the left of the narrow road, the tangle of wild palms, thickets, and vines yielded to a sweeping pasture where a pair of brown and white spotted colts browsed in ankle-high grass. The hum of the compact's engine brought their heads up, ears pricked, tails swishing. They wheeled and raced the car for half a mile behind white-washed wooden fencing. Diana laughed aloud in delight. "You beauties, you! Devereau House must be just around the next bend . . ."

And it was. A huge trellis of iron-filigree marked the turning off of the private road. Diana braked, twisted the steering wheel, and flashed beneath the lacy, weathered arch. The long driveway bore through the shade cast by graceful weeping willows. Diana got a first glimpse through the trees, and then as the driveway curved gently, the whole of Devereau House rose across her vision.

She caught her breath softly. There were the acres-long sweep of front lawns and gardens, and the house . . . multi-storied, its expanse of glistening white gentled by soft green window shutters, the incredible twin chimneys, the long veranda tucked behind the towering white columns.

Diana followed the driveway on its circular bend around a mossy, lilypad pool, drew over and braked on the edge of the white gravel. A smile danced across her full-lipped mouth. She had the urge to leap out and dash up the broad, shallow flagstone steps to the veranda yelling Lucy's name. Instead, she opened the car door and got out as sedately as her excitement would permit.

Dressed for driving in a loosely comfortable skirt, blouse, and sandals, she was an extraordinarily attractive image, tall, leggy, her boldly-featured face with its large dark eyes lifted to look at the house, sunlight a glint of copper in her auburn hair. The silence of the house meant nothing to her, not yet.

As she hurried around the car, the front door of the house opened. An old man came out, moving

11

onto the veranda with a cane in his left hand to offset his limp. He was tall, thin, stooped, and very gray, dressed simply in brown slacks and a short-sleeved white shirt.

"Mr. Devereau?" Diana knew, from Lucy's descriptions, that it was Huxley Devereau, Lucy's father. With a flashing smile, she hurried up the veranda steps.

But her smile faltered as she saw the way he was looking at her. In cavernous sockets, his eyes were brooding, haunted. They seemed to measure her, against questions of which she had no knowledge.

"You must be Diana." Once, his face had been that of a handsome, fine-boned patrician, the kind that brought waiters in exclusive restaurants to instant alacrity. He would have ridden his cane fields with a ramrod back on a spirited, high-stepping thoroughbred, and bankers would have arranged appointments at his convenience. But now the hair, brushed back in soft waves from blue-veined temples and a high forehead, had thinned and turned to silver, and the face was a gray parchment mask, with hollow cheeks and wrinkles threaded within wrinkles.

"Welcome to Devereau House," he added. "We'll have someone bring up your things. But I wanted to greet you myself. I've watched the drive-way for the past hour."

He reached to grip the fingers of her right hand. His touch was cold, like brittle onionskin. "Forgive me, Diana, but I wanted to be the first to look you over. Now I'm satisfied. I think you are everything Lucy said. I believe you will do."

"Do?" Diana stared at him in bewilderment.

He dropped her hand and stirred, moving toward the huge front door, which he'd left ajar. "I tried to reach you when you telegraphed from Wichita, but you were en route."

Diana stopped, still staring at him. "Lucy and I planned this visit almost a year ago. After I left Bankhead's Crossing and knew when I would arrive, I wired ahead from Witchita so I wouldn't burst in unexpectedly. Are you . . . telling me I shouldn't have come?"

"Dear God, no!" he husked. Again he caught her hand. This time his grip caused her to wince. "Anything but that! You're Lucy's dearest friend. I would have sent wild horses to bring you here. But I wanted to prepare you, when you wired that you were on your way."

A shard of ice seemed to steal into the sunlight. Diana felt as if her lips and mouth were drying out. "Prepare me for what, Mr. Devereau? Is Lucy ill?"

"I wish it were that simple," he said heavily. "Lucy suffered an accident, several weeks ago. She was hospitalized, in intensive care. The doctors did all they could, and now," his eyes labored toward the doorway, "we have brought her home and fitted out a room for her."

13

A torment of questions stormed through Diana's reeling mind, so many that she couldn't find words for a moment.

Huxley Devereau turned his head to look at her once more. A burning plea was in his eyes. "Now that you're here, pray God your presence will be a miracle medicine for Lucy . . ."

"But what happened to her?" Diana managed.

The old man hesitated. "The impossible," he said at last with a miserable shake of his head. "A stone statue toppled . . . fell on her . . . broke her spine . . ."

Diana's knuckles flew to her mouth. Her cheekbones thrust white. She fought a moment of faintness.

"Is Lucy . . ." She couldn't speak the rest of it.

"Her mind seems clear. Her eyes follow every movement within their range. She can move her right hand a little. Otherwise," Huxley Devereau choked on the bleak words, "Lucy is totally paralyzed . . ."

Chapter 2

And so Diana entered Deverau House, not as she had dreamed, but fighting the hysterical urge to laugh crazily and sob wildly. On the surface she was cool and self-possessed, and she fought against the bitter thought of how everything had changed in one instant. Happiness to horror . . .

Obeying Huxley's gesture, she quietly preceded him into the overwhelming spaciousness of an entry hall. Its curved, cathedral ceiling was two stories high. Antique marble-topped tables here and there were graced by vases of fresh flowers. The parquet flooring had the satin sheen that comes from years of meticulous care. On the walls were the colors of landscapes in oils, framed in hand-carved walnut. Upper-story hallways formed railed galleries overlooking the grand hall, accessible by a wide stairway with a heavy balustrade that curved upward.

Diana's eyes stung. Devereau House was even more than Lucy had described.

"If you'd like to freshen up first . . ." Lucy's father was saying.

"No!" Diana's response was quick. She took a breath to calm her voice. "I'd like to see Lucy right away, if it's all right."

The old man nodded. It was what he had wanted from her.

He started up the stairway, Diana at his side. Gripping his cane in one hand and the polished bannister with the other, he went up with a surprising vigor. Glancing at him, Diana suspected that he still had depths, and fire. He wasn't all worn husk. There was still a hint of headstrong arrogance in the thrust of his bony chin.

He paused at a heavy wooden-paneled door in the upper hall. Tilting his ear close to the door, he knocked softly.

The door opened noiselessly, revealing a tall, spare woman of advancing years. Her old-fashioned black dress accented her flat-chested plainness. Her face was a colorless, angular composition with a thin line for a mouth, a pointed nose, and sharp gray eyes. Her hair was like a casting of iron, drawn tight across her head and bunned at her nape. Spectacles dangled from her neck on a delicate golden chain, and she held an opened book pressed against her side.

She accounted for Diana with a swift, sharp

appraisal and spoke to the old man. "Yes, Mr. Devereau?"

"This is Miss Diana Latham."

"I know," the woman said. "Lucy's friend." Then a miracle of transformation flowed through the austere, frigid face as her lips curved in a gentle smile. She shifted her book and reached for Diana's hand. "I'm Clotilde Mathis, Diana. Cloty to my friends."

"Yes," Diana nodded. "I should have known you. Lucy spoke of you often."

"I was the governess who raised her," Cloty said. She had a nasal, Cajun-accented voice that brooked no argument. She glanced briefly at Huxley Devereau. "I returned to Devereau House after all these years in the ambulance that brought Lucy home from the hospital. The expensive, round-the clock RN's can check the pulse and measure the blood pressure—but Lucy needed her Cloty."

"Is she awake?" Huxley asked.

Cloty nodded. "I was reading to her." She looked directly into Diana's face. The gimlet gray eyes seemed to drill deeply. "Are you quite prepared, my dear?" she asked gently.

Diana nodded, not speaking. Cloty moved aside, and Diana took a first faltering step into the room.

It was a large, sunny room that had once known a canopied bed, frilly dressing table, fringed boudoir chairs, a little girl's doll collection and sorority picture when the girl was older. But the past had been removed, sterilized away to make way for a hospital room. There was a stainless steel table arrayed with medicines and the gleaming bulk of a steam sterilizer. There was a squat refrigerator, and a tall dolly to dangle bottles of liquid for intravenous intake. And there was the monstrous horror of a bed, with steel framing about it and pulleys and cords that meant traction for periods of perhaps each day.

But no matter, Diana thought wildly, the slender figure on the bed couldn't feel the weighted pull on limbs and spine . . .

Somehow she was moving, keeping herself from crumpling to her knees at the bedside.

She looked down at the small form, the pale, gamin face, the jet black hair fanned on the pillow, and the large, dark eyes, which filled with tears as they lifted to Diana's face.

Struggling, Lucy forced a small movement with her right hand, and Diana reached quickly to clasp the slender fingers.

"Hi," Diana said huskily. "I told you I would come. Here I am. We'll have hours together every day."

Lucy's eyes grew smoky.

"I know," Diana said. "It's not the vacation we planned. But we're together again. That's what counts."

Distantly, Diana heard the click of the door as Cloty and Huxley Devereau shut themselves out in the hall, respecting the privacy of the reunion.

Lucy's eyes were desperate with the effort to say something. The pathetic helplessness of it caught at Diana's throat.

Diana glanced about the room. Near the bed was a tall-backed rocking chair where Cloty no doubt sat when she read to Lucy. Beside the chair was a small table piled with books, with which the RN's would while away long hours of vigil. But there were no writing materials, no paper, no pencil or pen that Lucy might hold awkwardly in her right hand.

It wouldn't work anyway, Diana thought as she felt the weakness and nerveless quality of Lucy's fingers. Lucy couldn't hold a pen with sufficient strength and control to write a message. The others—Cloty, Lucy's father, the nurses— surely must have thought of the same thing. The absence of writing materials meant that the effort, the experiment, had failed.

Then an inspiration glinted in Diana's eyes. She bent a little closer.

"Lucy! Remember the old Indian custom . . . the way the Iaxtacans sometimes used a sign instead of a word? We picked up a good bit of it during our two years. Try, Lucy . . . tell me something with your hand!"

Diana let Lucy's fingers slip free and watched them intently. Lucy's hand moved. But the gesture was feeble, faltering. She repeated the vague, uncertain sign, a mist of perspiration dusting her wan cheeks from the effort. The signal still had no meaning for Diana.

It was useless, and Diana gently pressed her hand over Lucy's to stop the struggle.

"Okay," Diana said, "but we're still going to talk—if it takes all summer. You with it? Blink once for yes, twice for no."

Lucy blinked a ready yes. A spark of eagerness shone in her eyes. At least, Diana thought, it will give her something to do. It will be therapy of a sort. Pitiful little therapeutic project . . .

Diana reached and drew the rocking chair closer to the bed. She sat down and placed her hand, open palm upward, conveniently beside Lucy. Then she lifted Lucy's right hand and placed it against her palm.

"Now this is the gig," Diana instructed. "We'll spell out the words, letter by letter. I'll start saying the alpabet. When I reach the letter you want, peck a finger on my palm. Then I start the alphabet all over and when I arrive at the second letter of the word you have in mind, peck again. So it will take time just to say hello. We've plenty of time. We'll learn to short-cut, abbreviate, leave out prepositions and the like. Pretty soon you'll be able to tell me gossip about the nurses. Okay?"

Lucy blinked rapidly in excitement. Already, it seemed to Diana, there was a fresh hint of color in Lucy's cheeks.

"Now for the trial run," Diana said. "Got a word in mind?"

Lucy blinked yes.

Watching Lucy's hand as it rested on hers, Diana began the alphabet in slow rhythm. "A . . . B . . . C . . . D . . ."

Lucy's middle finger flicked quickly.

"D? The letter D?" Diana asked.

Lucy blinked her eyes once. Yes.

"Are you trying to say my name?"

Lucy's eyelids signaled a no.

Diana drew in a breath. "Okay. Second letter. A . . ."

Lucy tapped her palm.

"DA . . ." Diana said. "Now for the third letter, first word. A . . . B . . . C . . . D . . . E . . . F . . . G . . . H . . . I . . . J . . . K . . . L . . . M . . . N . . ."

Lucy's finger stopped her there.

"D-A-N . . ." Diana said. "Someone named Dan?"

Lucy blinked no, her eyes irritant with impatience for Diana to get on.

Gradually the full word took form. D-A-N-G-E-R.

Diana's brow knotted. A crawly feeling went

21

through her nape. "Danger . . . to someone in this house?"

Lucy blinked a yes. Her finger fluttered against Diana's palm. Clearly Lucy had more to say, a statement that couldn't be made with a simple yes or no response.

Diana pressed against the bed, a chill creeping through her as the message was laboriously spelled out. Her own voice began to seem disembodied as she endlessly repeated the alphabet to Lucy's stopping points.

"Danger . . . Evil . . . You must leave this place . . ." Diana whispered at last. Slowly, she lifted her eyes to Lucy's. Lucy was staring at her with a feverish brightness.

At that moment, the door clicked open, and Diana's head snapped around.

Wearing a crisp green nurse's uniform, a stalwart looking woman had entered. She crossed the room with a brisk, starched rustling. She had brown hair, quick hazel eyes, and an expressionless face.

"How do you do, Miss Latham," she said. "I'm Nurse Abernathy, I trust you had a good visit."

Diana rose stiffly, feeling a pulse still beating in her throat from Lucy's warning. "Yes, Lucy and I have been talking."

"Talking?" Miss Abernathy raised cool brows.

"A code . . . something we made up."

"That's intriguing." The nurse interposed herself between Diana and the bedside. She touched Lucy's wrist with practiced fingers.

"She told me . . ." Diana began.

"I'm really not interested, Miss Latham." The words cracked brittlely. "I'm concerned only with the welfare of my patient. Right now her pulse rate is at a dangerous level. You will have to leave."

"But I . . ."

"Please, Miss Latham! I'm sure your intentions were the best, but you've done enough damage for one day." With the efficient movements of a machine the nurse was crossing the room, taking a hypo syringe from the sterilizer while she gave her bedridden patient a look of quick concern.

With a flush of guilt, Diana gave Lucy a glance that was meant to be bracing. Then she turned and slipped softly from the room.

Half an hour later, Diana was in a room of her own, shown there by a pleasant middle-aged manservant named Lafarge. He had brought her luggage up during Diana's visit with Lucy.

Alone, Diana took a turn about her new quarters. It was a lovely suite, with a bath and dressing room, a small alcove sitting room, and a large bedroom furnished with French provincial. The windows overlooked a side lawn and miles of bayou, swamp, and mangrove jungle. The long view was one of primitive beauty, but Diana shivered slightly as he let the heavy lace curtain fall back over the window.

Danger . . . evil . . .

Why did Lucy want her to flee Devereau House even before she was unpacked?

Diana drew a long, heavy breath, casting a look at her suitcases and cosmetic kit stacked neatly at the foot of the bed. If she obeyed Lucy, she'd carry the bags back to the car.

Her mouth tightened. Without hesitation she swung an overnighter onto the bed and flipped it open. Some hard questions were forming in her mind about Lucy's "accident," and the answers were right here in Devereau House.

She was arranging lingerie in the chest of drawers when knuckles rattled in a blithe staccato on the door. Closing the drawer, Diana turned. Before she could cross the room, the door cracked, and a dark, tousled, rather shaggy head thrust in.

"Hi, in there. Getting settled?"

The head thrust around the door in Diana's direction. It was young, rawboned, with broad, white teeth revealed as the lips parted in a smile.

"I'm Antoine Devereau. Just drove in from the village and heard you'd arrived."

He came in without invitation, a tall, lank figure wearing muddy brogans, faded jeans, and a tattered brown knit shirt, clothing that made him studiedly, deliberately Cajun. His anti-Establishment uniform, Diana thought.

24

In Iaxtaca, Lucy had giggled a warning about her brother Tony: "He's two years older, but he always seemed a kid, even to me. Brash and hot tempered, like the old-time Devereaus. Papa spoiled him, I think. Village girls would swim an alligator bayou to keep a tryst with him. He'll aggravate you one minute and dope you with his smile the next. He's . . ." Lucy had sighed fondly. "Well, he's Tony."

Drifting across the room, he looked Diana over with brash appreciation.

"Lucy said you were lovely," he remarked boldly. A grin tugged his lips. "She needn't have understated the facts."

His manner might have been slightly offensive, except for his easy and genuine friendliness.

Diana couldn't help returning his smile. "With Lucy, who needs a press agent?"

He slouched into a brocade chair, watching her unpack. "How about I borrow a lot of your time this summer?"

The summer. It was a sobering thought. "Lucy will need a lot of my time," Diana said.

Turning, she glimpsed his face in the dressing table mirror. For a moment, his eyes were pools of shadows. A hardness stamped his face. The instant fled swiftly, but while it had lasted he had been cruelly mature, darkly dangerous.

Then he was smiling at her again, with a subdued air of boyish chastisement.

"Thanks for that," he said. "Thanks for putting Lucy ahead of everything else."

She thrust a blouse without care into the drawer she'd opened, turning toward him. "Tony, what happened to Lucy? Why? How? Where?"

The smile wiped from his lips. He studied her, then swung to a standing position. "Would you like to see the place?"

"Very much."

"Then come along."

Tony led the way down a narrow, gloomy rear stairway. They came out onto sunny rear grounds designed for relaxation and play. Umbrella-shaded tables and chairs were scattered between the house and a mirror-like swimming pool. Off to the left was a stone barbecue pit. Further away was a doubles tennis court. Beyond that, adjacent to a fenced riding ring, the stables and barn were vivid splashes of red against the distant, encroaching swampland.

"This way," Tony said.

They followed a flagstoned path off to the right, past the hulk of a triple garage. Tony set a brisk pace.

About five hundred yards from the house stood a weather-stained structure of solid stone, dreary, grim, ivy-grown. It was without windows, its front broken by an iron grillwork double-door that was rusted black from age.

Tony paused briefly. "The family mausoleum,"

he explained, flicking a thumb at the blocky pile of stone. "Down here we bury our dead above ground. You die, you are reverently slid into a crypt. Then maybe fifty years later your bones are shoved to the rear to make room for another decendent. Some of the crypts in there contain the dust of half a dozen Devereaus."

Diana drew back from the darkness beyond the iron-grilled doorway. It reminded her too quickly of the cramped darkness of a closet in a Kansas farmhouse. Her foster father had believed firmly in the corrective powers of that closet.

"You've been a bad child, Diana . . ." "I didn't mean it, papa . . ." "When you have confessed your badness and decided to be a good girl, you can come out, Diana . . ."

"Anything wrong?"

Diana started as Tony touched her arm. He was frowning as he looked at her.

She shook her head, wrenching her mind from the childhood memories. "No, I'm all right."

"Are you sure? You look absolutely pale."

"It's nothing," Diana said, turning from the sight of the Devereau mausoleum. "Do we have much further to go?"

"It's just a short way."

Tony continued to slip a puzzled glance at her as they moved into the shadows of tall pine trees. The pathway was shaded, cooler, carpeted with brittle, fallen pine needles. The mausoleum and

27

Devereau House had slipped from sight when they came upon a glade spangled with shafts of sunlight.

In the middle of the clearing stood the vine-grown ruins of a small stone building. Most of its tile roof had broken away, leaving gaping holes. The wooden windows and doors had rotted to nothing.

Touching her elbow to guide Diana forward, Tony said, "It's the remains of a chapel another Antoine Devereau built almost a hundred years ago. His young wife was thrown from a horse and killed on this very spot. He built the chapel to her memory. Sunday services were held here, as long as that Antoine Devereau lived, for the Devereaus and the plantation workers."

The tragic and touching little story caused Diana to look with interest at the ruins. She and Tony pushed dangling vines aside, picking their way through the yawning door.

The place was now all silence and decay, with scanty and stunted weeds pushing through cracks in the stone floor and a tall stone statue lying in broken pieces, face down, near the ruins of the altar. But in her imagination Diana could reconstruct the crude wooden pews and fill them with unknown, long-dead faces. Rapt and serious, they would have heard warnings of a fiery hell from the pulpit and sung a hymn while an adolescent boy manfully pumped an organ.

Tony was moving forward slowly, a drawn expression gradually etching his face as he looked at the broken statue and lifted his eyes to the tall niche in the weathered wall from which it had tipped and fallen.

"This is where it happened." His voice was a husky whisper. A muscle quivered in his lean jaw. His hand stole to Diana's. He gripped her fingers as if she would need to borrow of his strength.

"The Peace Corps experience made a deep impression on Lucy," he said. "After she returned home and it was all behind her, it seemed to grow in her mind, the poverty she had seen, the hard facts of life she had witnessed."

"I know," Diana murmured. "No one can work for two years in a village like Iaxtaca and come back unchanged."

He glanced at her. "You had your work. You were lucky on that score. It was a fresh challenge. Lucy had a lot of time to think and questions spawned in her mind like cells dividing. She would come here to meditate, to find solitude, to try and figure out some of the answers. The statue—the broken image is that of St. Joan—was Lucy's favorite of all the works of art we have around Devereau House. One evening . . ."

His words broke. His rawboned face was so drawn that it had the aspects of an old skull, but his eyes were those of a suffering boy. Diana looked at him with compassion.

29

"One evening," he resumed, a gravel in his voice, "Lucy didn't show for dinner. We came looking, my father, Philip Lockridge—whom you haven't met—myself, and several of the servants. It was I who found Lucy. Her broken body was lying there . . . beneath the toppled statue of her beloved St. Joan . . ."

Diana's impulse was to turn and hurry away. The chapel ruins held an ugly chill. She felt stifled by the decay, the baleful shadows. Her mind tormented itself with that earlier, tragic scene . . . Lucy, an almost childlike figure, kneeling there before the crumbling altar, the tall statue tilting and swooping from its niche as if it would embrace Lucy in its stony arms . . .

Diana felt the steadying pressure of Tony's arm about her shoulders. Her vision cleared, leaving before her the broken St. Joan in stone, the empty recess in the wall where it had stood.

She forced some strength into her knees, feeling Tony's supporting arm leave her slowly.

"Okay?" he asked.

She nodded.

"I shouldn't have brought you here," he said.

Turning a little from the sight of the broken statue, she glimpsed his rawboned face. What was he, really? A branch scorning the family tree with shaggy hair and swamp-mucker's attire?

He didn't seem so right now. His face was dark with concern for her, and his eyes were gentle.

Right now, he was altogether Lucy's brother, with Lucy's compassion and empathy.

"Don't feel bad, Tony." She managed a weak smile. "I had to see the chapel some time or other."

She didn't say the rest of it, that it seemed strangely fitting for this quiet and gentle Tony to have been the one to allow her here. His presence was the proper one beside her in this moment.

Their eyes met and held. Neither said anything. And then she sensed a subtle change. She felt his withdrawal. His lips thinned in an artificial smile, and his eyes shaded with a glint of derision for the barbs of an awry world. He seemed anything but quiet and gentle.

He flicked her playfully under the chin with a fingertip. "Let's not get sticky with this mutually comforting bit."

She brushed his hand aside with unintended force, thinking that she had really liked the Tony of a moment ago.

"Afraid of a little honest sentiment?" she tried to make the words a quip.

"Sentiment? Or sentimentality?" He thrust his fingers in the pockets of his faded jeans. "I think the latter stinks. Talk is cheap. Too often the guy who blows his paycheck in a ginmill can weep in his beer about how much he loves his wife and kids."

He sounds, she thought, as if his shield is really

a scar. She turned away, a little angry with herself for the way his shifting moods could affect her, even in the brief time she'd known him.

She didn't know whether she'd end up admiring Tony or condemning him. She knew already that he withheld his inner self. It would take time to descry the real Tony.

But one thing was sure. Theirs were personalities that struck sparks from the first hello. There'd never be bland neutrality between them.

Stepping carefully around the broken pieces of St. Joan, Diana moved closer to the wall niche where the statue had stood.

She felt the weight of Tony's intent gaze.

"You're wondering if it really was an accident," he said.

"Was it, Tony?"

"Why do you ask that?"

She hesitated, then plunged: "Lucy knew that if I stayed I would ask questions. If I asked questions, I would be in danger. For my sake, she asked me to leave."

"Lucy did what?" His words exploded an echo from the tumbledown walls.

"In code," Diana said quickly, turning toward him. He was staring at her with mouth agape.

"A little thing we worked out with finger taps," she explained.

"Oh . . . I see." His shoulders slumped. "For a second there you almost had me hoping your appearance worked one of those medical miracles and helped Lucy find her tongue. But this isn't a day of miracles, is it?"

"Maybe we're too busy looking the other way to discern them."

He kicked at a bit of debris. "Hogwash," he said. Looking up, he drifted to her side. "But you watch out for the miracle while I keep a baleful eye on reality. Meantime, we can stick to our common interest in Lucy."

"Truce accepted," Diana said agreeably.

He studied her closely. "Lucy reveal anything else in this tappy-tap code?"

"No," Diana said. "Just the hint that the statue didn't fall all by itself."

A tautness crept through Tony's dark face. It lent a saturninity, a look of wolfish threat. His eyes pierced the empty niche.

"I've asked myself the same question," he confessed. "And a dozen others. Why did the statue pick that moment to fall? Was it too bizarre to have been an accident?"

Watching him with a sidelong glance, Diana waited, knowing that he would reveal his own answers without prodding. She could sense the pressures the questions had built up in him.

Leaning forward, he picked up bits of dust from the base of the niche. He watched himself worry the grime between his fingertips.

"Rotten," he said in a half-whisper. "Decayed

mortar—like so many things around Devereau House . . ." He punctuated his murmur with a small, bitter laugh; and slowly wiped the dust on the leg of his jeans.

Once more his attention centered on the empty recess. "With the mortar rotted, the statue was doomed. St. Joan was certain to fall sooner or later. The moment was inevitable—and Lucy chose that moment to be here."

"A moment in which another person saw an evil opportunity?" The words slipped from Diana tightly.

Tony's hard-eyed gaze picked over every bump, crack, and brown viny twig in the niche. "It's possible Lucy stubbed a toe on a little vine trailing from the statue. With St. Joan teetering and ready to go, it would have been enough."

"Then you rule out a second person?"

"It had to be an accident," he said with a small note of anguish. "It was too bizarre not to have been an accident. Lucy hadn't an enemy in the world. No one stood to gain anything. She wasn't a threat to anybody. A second person implies a motive. Big motive. Strong enough for attempted murder. But there wasn't any motive."

"We don't always recognize or know our enemies, Tony."

He shot her a grim look. "Okay. But would Lucy supinely kneel there and wait for someone to climb up and tip St. Joan over?"

The set of his face reproached Diana. He's haunted by his own doubts, she thought, the chance that Devereau House spawned a would-be murderer.

But the greater anguish was Lucy's, Diana reminded herself. Imagine the unbearable pain if Lucy were lying helpless and mute knowing that the monstrous thing had been done to her deliberately, perhaps even suspecting who had done it.

"Someone could have tugged one of those vines you mentioned," Diana said insistently.

"While Lucy simply watched? Stood meekly as the statue toppled?" His tone was barbed, as if he'd asked himself all the elementary questions a dozen times over.

Diana slipped a glance about the chapel ruins. What Tony implied was true. A second person couldn't have entered the chapel and blithely conducted a ritual designed for murder without Lucy's awareness. And an aware Lucy wouldn't have taken it like a paralyzed chicken. Not the spunky gamin who'd taken on all the rigors of Iaxtaca.

Her gaze drifted down to that sickening focus, the broken pieces of St. Joan. "Were there signs of a struggle, Tony?"

"Do you mean she might have been hit over the head, positioned while she was unconscious, a target for the statue?"

"Something like that."

His dark brows quirked loftily. "We Cajuns aren't total morons, Miss Latham!"

"Tony, I didn't mean . . ."

"We are Devereaus, remember. We rate. We had not only the services of Constable Comage, the local law, but experts from New Orleans. Including a doctor of forensic medicine. Nothing indicated a struggle."

He snapped the words off like the closing of a book. But she guessed a reason for his temper. He wanted to accept the answers fully and be satisfied; but something in him held back, and he dreaded the thought of alternative answers.

He was moving restlessly now, bending a knee, reaching out as if he would touch the chipped stone of St. Joan's shoulder, drawing his hand back.

"Even at that," his lips twisted bitterly, "Lucy might be counted lucky. She lives—and as long as there is life there is hope of healing. Other Devereau women have been less fortunate. They have a habit of dying young, starting with one killed so long ago on this very spot."

And including your own mother, Diana thought. A shiver raced through her. Her mind was filled with a flash of memory . . . the village Iaxtaca . . . Lucy talking one rain-drenched night about her beautiful young mother with everything to live for, driving her car out alone and dying in a grinding accident . . .

Tony rose to full height, looking downward to watch his foot crush a clod. "Consecrated ground," he sneered. "That fool . . . that first Antoine Devereau . . . that builder of chapels. Consecrated it to the devil, if you ask me!"

A dryness worked in Diana's throat. "Tony, I think I'd like to go now."

His head jerked up. He lifted his right hand and brushed the back of it across his forehead. His eyes cooled with a smoky film. Then he nodded.

He touched her elbow lightly as they started threading their way out, along a weedy aisle between the rotted and sagging pews.

They moved several paces in silence, picking their steps. A breeze, touched with a faint peatlike smell, stirred from the swamp, rustling the upper limbs of trees that towered outside over the jagged, broken chapel walls.

Then without warning, Tony's fingers clamped tight on Diana's arm. Before she could make a startled outcry, he pressed a finger across her lips, commanding silence.

He stood with muscles in quick strain, head half turned, listening with the keen ears of the swampland native.

"Hear that?" he whispered. "Could be a frightened old coon rustling in a thicket——or someone spying on us. I think I'll have a look-see."

Diana was suddenly standing alone as he slipped away cat-like. His quick, supple movements brought the fleeting thought to her of the sinewy young hunters of Iaxtaca.

He was a shadow swishing silently through a shaft of sunlight; then he'd vanished beyond the scabrous wall.

Ears straining, Diana eased in his wake, carefully quiet. She jerked up short and caught a breath as Tony yelled outside. The sound was smothered in the furious thrashing of underbrush. The explosive struggle was punctuated by Tony's snarls and the hoarse yelps of a second man.

Diana ran toward the chapel entrance. As she burst outside, a man rounded the corner of the building in full flight, throwing a look over his shoulder. In his right hand he was carrying a piece of fallen tree limb which he'd grabbed for a makeshift club during his flurry with Tony.

Not seeing or hearing Tony, Diana endured a frightening thought. But even as the question of Tony's safety shot through her, the stranger turned his head and saw her standing alone and helpless in the wash of sunlight.

The sight of her broke his stride. Then he came on in a fast, shuffling gait, a gaunt figure raising the length of dead tree limb with a long, bony arm. "Get out of my way, gal!"

Diana stood rooted during an instant of numbing fright. She was aware of his club, and of him as a rawboned old figure as gray and tough as

38

weathered cypress, his dirty clothes flapping like the rags of a scarecrow.

But it was the sight of his face that loomed stronger than any other detail. Sunken-cheeked, sallow, lantern-jawed, the features were an arrangement in the grotesque. During some horrible moment in the past, the right side of his face had been smashed. The crushed bones and tissues had knitted back wthout competent medical care, probably none at all. The result was a misshapen gargoyle with everything pushed to the left, the sharp chin, the long, pointed nose, the lumpish, twisted cheekbone.

Fighting a faintness, Diana stumbled aside. Almost upon her, the old man reeled to the left, away from her. He lowered the club, shifting it to his other hand. Oddly set in his out-of-kilter face, his gray eyes flicked a glance. The unbroken side of his scar-tissued mouth formed words: "Smart of you to give an old man room, Miss. I'm obliged."

He plunged along the face of the chapel and through a break in the trees, the drumming of his footsteps quickly fading.

Drawing a quavering breath, Diana discovered that she was trembling. Her teeth gritted in impatience with herself. Resolutely, she moved toward the corner of the chapel where the nightmarish old man had appeared.

Calling out Tony's name, she heard a mumbled

reply. She almost collided with him as she rounded the angle of the ruined walls. He was a groggy figure on uncertain feet, looking at her owlishly.

At his side, she flung a supporting arm about his waist, her eyes measuring the damage revealed by a slight swelling on his left forehead.

She looked about for a place where he could lie down, but he was steadying up on his own two feet. He raised his hand and winced as he touched the bruise on his forehead, but he managed a wry grin.

"That was no human," he said drily, "but a shaggy old swamp panther."

"Tony . . ."

"Imagine me . . ." his grin became a good-natured laugh, "at first thinking I shouldn't hurt the old boy. Some old boy! Still, I'd have collared him, if he hadn't grabbed that hunk of deadwood during the rough and tumble."

"Tony, are you sure you're okay?"

The close up image of her face began to gather his attention. He studied her lips, her eyes. A warmth began to steal through her.

"My poor head's bashed in," he sighed. "You'll have to nurse me back to health."

His head was lowering, his lips about to touch hers. She slipped her arm from his waist and took a step aside, a little short of breath, feeling color suffuse her cheeks.

She gave a small laugh, sidetracking the personal direction the moment had suddenly taken. His moods were certainly anything but predictable.

"I think you'll survive," she said. "If you show signs to the contrary, I'll stay with Lucy. This should free nurse Abernathy to take care of you."

"Abernathy?" He shook his head dolefully. "You sure know the prescription to cure a fellow in a hurry, don't you?"

He took her hand in his, and the last vestiges of his unsteadiness seeped away as they started walking along the path in the direction of the manor house.

Birds were singing, and it was an ironically beautiful day, a beauty containing the heart-wracking sight of Lucy, a broken St. Joan, the frightful old man.

"Who was he, Tony?"

"The old fellow back there?" Tony raised fingertips to the small puffiness on his forehead as if his memory had a special spot for the old man for a long time to come. "His name is Ozar Fant."

"Ozar Fant," Diana mused. "That's a strange name."

"Cajun country," Tony reminded. "Lot of things here would seem strange to an outsider. Fant's way of life, for one thing. He just drifted in sometime in the recent past and took up squatter's possession of an abandoned shack on Bayou le Chat. He can fish, trap, hunt, live off the land to keep body and soul together."

"Sounds grim."

Tony glanced at her as they rounded a curve in the path. "Could be. Could also be the greatest mode of life, if you're so disposed, free, simple, uncomplicated. But in Fant's case, I'm not sure he doesn't augment his livelihood by pilfering. This is the third—no, the fourth—time I've caught him skulking around Devereau House."

"Maybe he's too perversely proud to beg, Tony."

"Maybe."

Diana was thoughtful while they covered a few yards. "Or lonely. Wanting the sight of other people. Tired of hiding that pitifully wrecked face off in the swamp."

Tony made a sound resembling a snort. "Don't waste your sympathies. Fant told a bragging tale in the village about a big bull alligator doing that to his face. He was a poacher, dealing in black market alligator hides. Dirty, rotten, illegal business—and it's wiping out the last of the alligators."

Diana noted the rising heat in his voice. He doesn't like the idea of the swamp lying lifeless, its creatures extinct, she thought.

Tony drew a temper-cooling breath. "Anyway, seems that Fant shot this big bull 'gator, thought he was dead, and went into shallow water to drag the carcass out. The dying beast had one last explosion left in his tail, the deadliest weapon of an

42

alligator. Fant took the blow across the side of his face. His head and shoulders were slammed onto the bank. He didn't drown. He crawled off and nursed his wounds. His survival proved him a little tougher than the alligator."

Tony slowed, stopped, taking both Diana's hands in his. With rivulets of bright sunlight spilling through the trees, they stood in the pathway facing each other. She was held more by the darkness in his eyes than by his touch.

"Let's hope," he said thinly, "that Ozar Fant is nothing more than a sneak thief. Otherwise . . . what keeps luring such a man back to Devereau House?"

The shocks and dislocations of the past few hours spiraled to tight focus inside Diana. Tony's face, the trees, patches of sky all seemed a little unreal.

A dark certainty that Lucy was right crept through Diana's mind. She slipped a glance toward the manor. Danger House, she thought.

She was surprised with her own outward steadiness as she turned and moved on, Tony beside her.

"I wish I could answer your questions, Tony. All of them."

"Forget it." He plucked a dead twig from a tree limb in passing and began crumbling it to smaller bits. "I didn't expect an answer. But it helps sometimes to put the questions in words."

Beyond breaks in the trees, chinks of white wall and towering chimneys took on definite outline.

Diana tried to recall the eagerness with which she had first looked at the house. Instead, she felt as if she were being tugged unwillingly forward.

I'm scared, she admitted in a lonely corner of her mind, and I'd like to put Lucy in the car and drive away.

But she walked quietly on.

She couldn't put Lucy in the car, and therefore she couldn't drive away.

Chapter 3

The woods, thickets, and family mausoleum fell behind. The backyard recreation area, pool, tennis court, barbecue, spread before Diana and Tony, suggesting that here at Devereau House life was carefree fun and play. The house towered in seeming white purity, symbol of security and gracious living.

Skirting the swimming pool at Tony's side, Diana thought: What an illusion . . . what liars material things can be . . .

Tony touched her arm, bringing Diana's glance. He was casting a glum look at a white Continental that had been parked in the driveway near the triple garage during their absence.

"I suppose they've come to dinner—to size you up, Lucy's friend."

She studied the luxurious car briefly as they moved along the patio.

"Belongs to my brilliant cousin," Tony said, thin-lipped, "Philip Lockridge."

Diana wondered if Tony always spoke of his cousin so coolly. "He was with you the night you found Lucy, wasn't he?"

"Practically. Big man. Organizing the search. Cautioning us all to keep our heads. We'd fanned out, my father, Philip, the servants, and I. He was the first of the others to burst into the chapel when I started yelling."

While Tony spoke, a wiry old woman shuffled onto the patio carrying a sudsy bucket. With a sparse nod at Diana and Tony, she set the pail beside one of the metal, umbrella-shaded tables. She lifted out a dripping sponge and started scrubbing. She appeared engrossed in the menial task, but Diana felt the sharpness of the old woman's covert appraisal.

Tony veered toward the table, where a film of wind-deposited dust was fast disappearing under the energies of the old woman's work-roughened hands.

"How are you, Myree?"

"I'll do," the old woman murmured.

Looking at her, Diana was reminded of a mangy old gray cat, a collection of bone and sinew stronger than leather and more durable than time itself.

It wasn't a pleasant analogy; Diana's fondness

46

for animals included cats, but not those with the slinky aura, the creepers, the stalkers.

This first impression sparked a flicker of guilt in Diana. Who knew the bitters of this old woman's years, the forces that had hammered her into what she was today? She couldn't help the wrinkle-shriveled face, the balding head with its small top-knot of rat-gray hair, the stealthy way she used her watery blue eyes, the feeling she imparted to a stranger that she was crouching within herself. It was possible that a lifetime ago she'd been as gaminly lovely and vivacious as the Lucy of the Peace Corps.

"This is Miss Diana Latham," Tony was saying.

"I know," Myree muttered.

"Diana, meet Myree." There was a touch of natural compassion in Tony's voice as he spoke to the old woman. "If you need fresh towels, Myree's the one to look for around here."

Diana caught the small way in which Myree shied from Tony. Maybe the wily old woman feared any hint of kindness.

Diana had extended her hand. "I'm glad to know you, Myree."

Myree shifted her sponge and wiped her palm on the front of her shapeless, faded cotton dress.

"Yes, Miss Latham." Myree clung to Diana's hand with curved, work-roughened talons while she craned her thin, wrinkle-wattled neck and

47

peered at Diana's face. "You are Lucy's dearest friend."

"Yes," Diana nodded, wishing she could gracefully break the handshake.

"Can you help her?" the scrawny old servant asked.

"I can try," Diana said.

Myree bobbed her head, releasing Diana's hand. As if satisfied with Diana's answer, the old woman dipped her sponge and resumed her methodical cleansing of the table. She was the tireless, robot-like menial.

Tony didn't move right away. "I see Philip's car over there. Did Robin Toutain arrive with him, Myree?"

Silently, Myree moved her head in the affirmative, not breaking the rhythm of her sponge.

"Well," Tony said. "I guessed Robin would."

He turned from the old woman, and Diana had to take a quick step to fall in beside him.

He by-passed the tall glass doors that separated the patio from the huge playroom, choosing entry through the same corner doorway that had let them out of the house.

They were halfway up the dim, back stairway before Diana broke the silence.

"Who is Robin Toutain, Tony?"

"Philip's private secretary, indefatigable girl Friday, constant shadow," he said brittlely, snapping off further discussion of the subject.

They emerged into the upper railed gallery. The house was very quiet, the spacious, tasteful luxury of the hallway below devoid of life. Then from some room off the main hall came the muffled, distant sound of a woman's laugh. It drifted up pleasantly, but the sound of it thinned Tony's lips. Diana wondered fleetingly if he were jealous of Robin Toutain and his cousin Philip.

At the doorway to her bedroom suite, Diana paused, looking up into Tony's face.

"I'm glad you showed me the chapel, Tony."

"Any time. Always glad to be of service."

"See you at dinner."

"Not tonight. I think I'll try the crabcakes at the village beanery." His voice was flat; and then one of those sudden shifts in mood glinted through him.

"Sometimes I seem to curdle Robin Toutain's appetite and take the edge off of Philip's," he added with a droll laugh. "Cook here makes the finest crayfish bisque in all Louisiana. Don't you want them to enjoy it?"

Grin flashing, he touched Diana softly on the cheek. "Anyway, I'd rather claim your time when I can have you to myself."

With that, he turned and set off along the gallery, breaking the quiet with a cheerful, off-key whistling.

Watching his departing figure turn onto the main hall stairway and descend from sight, Diana

49

shook her head in mild bafflement. In their moment of meeting, Tony had seemed as obvious as numbers written on a blackboard, a brash young man with perhaps too many material advantages.

Now, she wondered if the upshots of his maze-like personality didn't often surprise Tony himself.

In the solitude of her bedroom suite, Diana's spirit drooped. A reaction to the experiences of the past hours came over her like an entangling web.

She drifted pensively to the windows. The miles-long view of swamp, mangrove jungle, cane breaks, stands of heat-blasted pine and mangrove smudged in the distances reminded her of the isolation of Devereau House. She shivered slightly, turning away.

In the quiet, a sense of loneliness darkened her. Tears for Lucy stung her eyes. But mingled with the sorrow was a choking anger at the unfairness of the cruelty that Lucy, gentle Lucy, had suffered, was suffering.

Why had it happened? And how—if the stone St. Joan hadn't toppled from natural causes?

Myriad questions beset Diana like beating invisible wings. Where must she look? What should she look for?

Did a face in Devereau House mask incredible evil? Which one?

Diana sank onto a delicately modeled provincial boudoir chair, hands knotting in her lap. Like groping about a seven-gabled rooftop in the dark, she thought, I could touch some little fact or detail and not even realize it was dangerous . . .

Then she became aware of herself sitting here with head bowed and shoulders pinched. She pondered the self-image for a moment, in distaste. Color me self-pity, she thought wryly.

She pushed up from the chair, forcing her mind away from sadness, discouragement, despair.

Perhaps Lucy could tell her more. And that brought up the thought of Nurse Abernathy. The nurse had impressed Diana as a do-it-by-the-book robot, short of leniency with anyone who, in her view, meddled with the patient.

I'll manage Abernathy, Diana decided, if I must. One of the other nurses on the round-the-clock schedule might be more human and cooperative.

Until she could re-open communication with Lucy on an apparently innocent visit, Diana knew she must keep up appearances. Indulge in polite dinner table conversation. Take a swim. Stroll in the gardens. Have a breakfast on the patio.

And take the shivery risk of turning up the detail, the word, the nuance, that didn't fit . . .

At five thirty Diana went downstairs to meet Philip Lockridge and Robin Toutain. The curiosity that Tony had whetted about these people returned.

Seeing no one else in the great hall, Diana

51

paused. Then, hearing the filter of stereo music from the rearward part of the house, Diana decided they were out there, in the large playroom she'd glimpsed earlier from the patio.

She'd taken a few steps when Huxley Devereau spoke her name. She stopped and turned. The towering hallway divided the house into east wing and west, and the thin, silvery old man had entered from a room on the east. Double doors stood open behind him, giving Diana a glimpse of thickly carpeted floor, massive mahogany desk, and booklined walls.

Huxley closed the doors of the library-study, settled his cane in his left hand, and limped toward Diana.

With his patrician smile and courtly bearing, he looked far less haggard than he had earlier today, when he'd reflected the strain of waiting and watching for Diana to arrive, framing in his mind a hundred different ways of breaking the news about Lucy, uncertain as he'd stared at the long driveway of the reactions of Diana, a stranger.

His glance approved the attractive picture that Diana made in a modishly simple black dress, her auburn hair brushed to a lustrous coppery cascade to her shoulders.

With a small bow, the old man offered his arm. Diana linked her hand with the crook of his elbow. They strolled the hall, following the sound of the soft stereo music.

"My dear," he chuckled, "I envy Tony the company he kept this afternoon."

"He showed me . . ." Diana caught back mention of the ruined chapel, ". . . something of the grounds."

She felt the dart of Huxley's brief glance. She had the notion that he knew where she and Tony had gone and what had been said. But he nodded in casual fashion.

"It's the loveliest spot on earth to walk about." The very quiet of his voice revealed his attachment to this house, this land. "Sometimes I can stroll the gardens, the pathways, the shaded glens and bayous I explored as a boy, and feel almost as if I could throw the cane away."

Diana felt an undercurrent in his voice that was more revealing than his mere words. It expressed more than the regretful knowledge that, in his years, each passing day brought him that much closer to the final departure from Devereau House. It insinuated a remorse for things said and unsaid, acts done and not done in the dark recesses of the past.

But his smile held, lending benignity to the wrinkled gray parchment of his face. With a shifting of his cane, he reached to open a sliding door. It tracked as quietly as a curtain between the form old luxury of the rest of the house and a playroom where casualness was the keynote.

53

The furnishings were a carefree scattering of rattan and leather, chairs, tables, huge hassocks, couches. Potted miniature palms and poinsettias conspired with the sweep of glass in the outer wall to blend the room with the outdoors.

At a table in the further end of the room, a man and woman were engrossed in a card game. Diana assumed they were Philip Lockridge and Robin Toutain. She had a moment to study them before she and Huxley were observed.

Robin was an enviable portrait of cool blonde beauty, eyes and full red lips teasing in triumph as she drew a card and spread her gin-rummy hand.

"Gin!"

Philip gave her a mock glower. A rangy, wide-shouldered, conservatively-tailored figure, he looked as fit and vigorous as a collegiate quarterback. He turned his head, hearing Diana and Huxley approach, and stood up in a movement of quietly flowing power.

"Are we interrupting?" Huxley said.

"Gratefully," Philip smiled, "I'm still sixty cents ahead at this point."

The old man's hand folded over Diana's. "This is Diana Latham, Lucy's friend," he said with an unexpected fondness and pride. "Miss Robin Toutain, Lucy."

"Hi." Robin's smile was friendly, but Diana didn't miss the canny examination of Robin's violet eyes. I'll bet, Diana thought, she can even read the label in my dress.

"And my nephew, Philip Lockridge," Huxley was saying.

Diana felt her hand grasped by one of tensile strength. She looked up into a face that was firmly cut, evenly featured, a face born to command with an easy order, a quiet word, a nudging suggestion. Flecks of premature gray at Philip's dark brown temples caught the light as he nodded his approval.

"Our Lucy is given to overstatement, but not in your case," he smiled. "It's a pleasure we've looked forward to. Welcome to acadian country, Diana."

She met the depths of brown eyes warmed with interest. A pleasant pulse rippled through her. She tried to think of a bright response, but it came out a sincere and simple, "Thank you, Philip."

Robin had risen. Outwardly friendly, she linked her arm with Philip's. It was a subtle gesture of possession, an artful hint to Diana.

"We'll have to show Diana some of the historic sights and local pageantry, won't we, darling?" Robin asked, as if Philip, not she, would decide how and when he saw Diana in the days ahead.

Without waiting for Philip to agree, Robin continued, "We Cajuns," Robin's smile tolerated Diana as an outsider, "hold a festival at the merest excuse. Our old-world customs, costumes, communal dances delight the tourist who chances upon the goings-on. We're forever celebrating our rice crop, sugar cane, oil, fur trade, dairy products."

"Even the yams," Philip laughed, "with the Yambilee festival at Opelousas, which claims the title of yam producing capital of the world."

"You'll find us quaint," Robin promised.

Huxley cleared his throat. "How about a predinner cocktail to sharpen the taste buds? Do you like shrimp, Diana?"

"One of my favorites."

"Good! Tonight we'll have a jambalaya that'll reveal the purpose for which the shrimp was created!"

Even in his continual grieving concern for Lucy, the old man had an irrepressible gusto, part and parcel of his Cajun being. What a figure he must have once cut, Diana thought.

They sipped cocktails beside the pool while the most serene of all twilights crept over the far-flung swamps and bayous.

These were moments of pleasurable ease, but for the sense of grim incompletion, the want of Lucy's bright face and witty chatter.

To Robin's chagrin, Philip gave most of his attention to Diana during the casual flow of talk.

Diana was grateful for his presence. A rapport grew quickly between them. He understood the vacation-excitement that had been shattered to a sense of desolation. He was steady, solid substance in the lowering nightshade. He was quiet strength without the compulsive need to prove itself. He was an attentive listener, and an urge to laughter with a funny little story.

An errant sketch flipped through Diana's mind, of Philip taking her hand and drawing her to the protective tenderness of his arms.

With an inward giggle, she thought: I don't blame you, Robin! If he were mine, I'd be jealous too.

During the give and take of conversation, Diana learned that Philip was head of Nectar Sugar, a large refining and shipping operation. It was a staid, dependable business, its stock never offered for public sale.

A Lockridge of five generations ago had built the first sugar refinery not far from Devereau plantation. The expansion and development of the nation during the years after the Civil War had brought the company to the growth level it had long since retained, its assets including docks, warehouses, cargo riverboats, railroad sidings.

Philip's father had married Huxley Devereau's younger sister. Philip was the eldest of four children. By tradition and education, he had been pointed toward his present post from the time of his infancy. He had accepted, without rebellion or complaint, the responsibilities destined for his shoulders.

In her mind, Diana compared Philip and Tony. Philip the predictable, never-faltering engine . . . Tony of the uncertainties and whiplash moods. One of them with his hand firmly on the future, the other facing detours and chasms in the by-ways . . . One capable of decisive action, the other getting whacked with a club for his attempt to question an Ozar Fant.

Diana realized that Tony was getting the worst of it, and she was strangely angered with herself. After all, let's not be unfair to Tony . . .

When talk veered to Nectar Sugar, Robin was infused with fresh animation. Her knowledge of the business seemed as thorough as Philip's, and her ambitions stronger.

As she talked of new packaging methods, Philip watched her with affectionate respect. He drawled a remark now and then with a fondness stemming from life-long association and similarity of background.

Diana drew a mental picture of Philip and Robin squabbling as childhood neighbors, Robin leading the cheering as Philip punched out a high school football victory, Robin in Philip's convertible on the way to a college prom.

"We do everything at Nectar Sugar reasonably well," Robin finished in a rush, "except—we don't raise the cane."

"Robin," Philip murmured. "Not tonight."

Huxley raised a thin hand. The soft lights of the patio had been turned on, and in the glow the blue veins on the back of his hand traced a pattern against the tissue-thin skin.

"It's all right, Philip," he sighed. "Robin may well be right." He studied her dispassionately. "You'll never rest, my dear, until the merger of Nectar Sugar and Devereau cane lands is a fact."

Robin dropped her eyes demurely. "I'll always obey Philip's wishes and yours, Uncle Huxley."

"So long as those wishes are born in your lovely, golden head. And I'm not your uncle—yet." Huxley's indulgent laugh kept any trace of sting from his words. He glanced at Diana, eyes mischievous. "Do Kansas women maneuver their men so well? Down here, they're silken—a silken web—once a man gets in their hands."

"You'd think we are Jezebels, Diana," Robin laughed. "But if I've nagged these two, it's only for the welfare of the family. A merger would mean unit control of everything, from the cutting of the cane to the delivery to the store where the customer buys her sugar. Don't you think it sounds far more efficient?"

"Spare Diana involvement." Huxley settled in his canvas chair and stared at the light reflections on the glassy surface of the swimming pool. "It always boils down to one point. You'd streamline everything out here and turn the plantation into a machine."

His thin face, the wrinkles furrows of black in the gentle lighting, lifted slowly. He mused on the tiptop silhouettes of distant trees against the darkening sky. "It's always meant more than that. Some of the people out there were born on Devereau soil. They would have to go, if mechanization came. And that would hardly be right."

Robin leaned and laid the warmth of her hand on his. "Bless you, Uncle Huxley—but can the best intentions stop the changes that time brings?"

He shook his head mutely, shoulders sagging a little. "This is hardly the time or place, Robin . . . and I wouldn't make a merger move without a final talk with Tony."

"Of course," Robin murmured. "All this, for miles around us, is earmarked for him. But it we await Tony, the jungle will nibble away the fields and mold will creep over the house."

Philip cleared his throat. A soft sound, it had the authority of a master sergeant's bark. "We have a guest," he reminded. He stood up, offering Diana his arm. "How about we go in and fire the cook, if dinner isn't ready for the table? I'm famished."

Slipping an icy look at Diana, Robin rose gracefully. Her smile flashed for Philip. "You're right, darling. Do forgive us, Diana." Her bright glance was encompassing them all. "Uncle Huxley, would you escort a deserted woman in to dinner?"

As they strolled from the patio, Diana found herself with a perverse little thought: I wish Tony had stayed and positively wrecked her appetite . . .

Chapter 4

Cloty joined them at dinner, reporting that Lucy was resting well after the excitement of seeing Diana. The testy exterior shell of the aging governess, so easy to see through, succumbed to the spell of the candlelight and age-mellowed wood of the dining room. Her brusque humor enlivened dinner table repartee. One moment she was relating how Philip in the excitement of his first football game punted the ball straight into the derrier of his blocking halfback. The next, she might be lifting her spectacles on their neck chain and severely looking at a steaming dish or tureen as it was brought in.

Diana was seated at Huxley's right. Before her, the ponderous antique table was covered with white damask. The low centerpiece was of creamy magnolia blossoms. The array of crystal, bone china, and silver service was an everyday display of family heirlooms.

The piece de resistance was the shrimp jambalaya, and as Diana tasted the blend of succulent shrimp, rice and tangy creole sauce, she discovered a unique treat. The few jambalayas she'd previously tried in restaurants had been mere imitations.

Pleased by her reaction, Huxley, in the role of conversing host, mentioned the origins of the dish and the word.

"In the beginning it was a ham and rice dish," he explained. "Jambon, French for ham, and a la ya, a sort of African for rice."

From appetizer to Cajun coffee, which Cloty warned Diana "is best described as battery acid distilled from ground-up chickory," the dinner should have been the most pleasant of occasions.

But Diana sensed a vague undercurrent, of things unsaid, subjects skirted. She was nagged with the feeling that Devereau House was putting its best foot forward in an hospitable consideration of a respected guest.

Dinner over, Robin veered the talk back to the subject of a business merger.

She's as tenacious, Diana thought, as a soft little golden caterpillar attacking a mulberry tree.

"Have you had a chance to look about the house yet?" Philip asked, taking Diana's arm.

She shook her head.

"Then why don't we? If these two are determined to talk business?"

As Philip guided Diana off for the start of the tour, Robin called after them, "We really can't stay too late, darling. Remember your early appointment with the trade commissioner and the board meeting at ten in the morning."

During the next two hours, Diana absorbed the lore of Devereau House. Philip was a comforting presence, a reminder that stability and strength did exist in a world that had gone haywire with the first glimpse of Lucy. Beside him, Diana could almost relax as he told little stories that brought color and life to Devereau House.

In the music room with its fine old concert grand and chairs upholstered in gold cloth: "When he was young, Huxley would sometimes finish a roistering holiday in New Orleans, roaring up with a Dixieland band piled in a huge, open touring car. Neighbors would see the dust and start arriving. Field hands would congregate. Somebody would pull the stopper on the bathtub gin, and cook would start shoveling the food. Like, m'am, you've never heard such jam sessions!"

In the brocade and velvet of the living room: "Standing right on the marble hearth, Devereau girl married yankee captain on garrison duty after Appomattox. Having grown fond of the young fellow, her father rode the countryside for awhile with a shotgun across his saddle, in case anyone wanted to question or insult the marriage. Even so, the scandal lasted for a generation. She went north with her husband and never returned, and I suppose there's some Devereau blood still beating about New England."

Entering a dark doorway, Philip pressed a switch. A long, narrow room came to soft life. It was a small art gallery, with portraits in oil along the inner wall.

"Fellow there with the muttonchop whiskers," Philip said, tucking Diana's hand in the crook of his elbow, "had a fistfight on the floor of the Louisiana state legislature. And that lass with the beady eyes years later marched on same legislature, one of our early suffragettes."

While Philip talked, the portrait of a young and lovely woman caught Diana's eye. She was drawn toward it, Philip giving her a glance as he stayed at her side.

Diana's intent study of the picture held Philip silent. With jet black hair, large and sensitive dark eyes, slightly parted lips, the lifelike ivory-tinted face seemed to have been captured by the artist between gusty breaths.

A small shiver touched Diana. "It could be Lucy's face."

"Lucy's mother," Philip said.

Diana held Philip's arm a little more tightly. "The artist was a genius—but cruel."

"Cruel?"

"Beyond the contentment of her moment, he included something darkly haunted. Was she really like that, Philip?"

"I was very young," he said, "but I remember. Yes—she was like that."

Diana was spellbound, staring at the portrait. "What a cold, hollow place this house must have been when she was killed."

"It's never been quite the same since," Philip said gravely. "She was a very good driver. But that night . . . she went out and careened her car recklessly from Devereau House. When she stopped, the car was a twisted pile of junk. It took a wrecking crew and state highway patrolmen an hour to free her body from the wreckage."

"It sounds as if she did it deliberately, Philip. Rushing out, driving totally out of character. But why? She had everything, wealth, position, a family . . ."

Philip grasped her chin, turning her face toward his, breaking her gaze from the picture.

"It happened a long time ago, Diana. Let the past belong to Devereau House." His warm smile as he looked down into her face eased the gloom that the portrait had imparted to Diana.

"You've had a long, trying day," he said. "You

66

must be tired, and I've been thoughtless, dragging you about the house. We've plenty of time for grand tours."

Not until later, when the evening was over and she was on her way up to her room, did Diana realize how neatly Philip had evaded her question.

But it lingered in her mind. A lovely young woman, possessing everything that life could offer, didn't suddenly hurl herself to death without a desperate and damning reason.

Diana dragged to a halt in the upper hallway. Over the balustrade, she looked down into the vacancy of the grand hall. The lights had been lowered to murky dim, with shadows falling heavily. The silence was broken only by the sibilance of a muggy wind off the bayous.

In her tired, low state, Diana could imagine the snarl of a car's engine outside mingled with the laughter of shattered sanity as a young woman raced off to her death.

And now, a generation later . . . like mother, like daughter? A car in the first instance, a stone statue in the second?

An inward scream formed, and Diana was dizzy with the mind searing thought. No! She wouldn't entertain the satanic possibility for a second. Even if Lucy's mother had sought self-destruction, it didn't mean that Lucy was doomed to the same end. It was preposterous, this crazy notion that

Lucy in abject self-negation might have toppled the stone St. Joan onto herself . . .

Dry-throated, Diana turned from the view of the hallway below. She shook her head tiredly. Philip had been right earlier. It had been a hellish day, one of the worst of her life, leaving her prey to the strangeness and isolation of Devereau House.

Firmly, she walked on toward her suite. Then as she was about to open the door, she heard a small sound of movement inside.

She hesitated, frowning. Slowly she turned the knob and cracked the door.

She looked inside the bedroom and saw Myree, the wiry old menial Tony had introduced on the patio. Myree stood startled, muscles drawn like a time-scarred cat's, light catching on her thinning gray topknot.

Myree emitted a breath, her slatternly body relaxing as Diana entered the room.

"You give me a turn," Myree said a bit snappishly, "slipping the door open that way."

"And you gave me one," Diana laughed, "being in here this time of night."

Myree lifted bony fingers and touched the towels draped across her shoulder. "I brought you fresh towels." A thought crossed her mind. Beads of suspicious belligerence slipped into her watery eyes. Her mouth crimped, deepening the wrinkles cobwebbed about it.

"I reckon you'll tell Mr. Devereau I forget? Fresh linens twice a day is the rule, and I was supposed to see to it earlier, but it slipped my mind, with all what I have to do."

Like a bedraggled old bobcat, Diana thought, retreating up the nearest tree, to claw and spit at the hounds below.

Diana closed the door and moved across the room. "Why would I say anything to Mr. Devereau, Myree?"

"Well," Myree dropped her eyes, measuring Diana's distance by the toes of her shoes, "I reckon always on the worst of things."

The old woman repulsed and aroused pity in Diana in the same instant. But she was a figure who reached every corner and cranny of this house almost daily with her mops and dust cloths. And who noticed a menial any more than a stick of furniture? But a menial had eyes and ears . . .

Diana kept the opening ploy casual: "Do you come from this part of the country, Myree?"

"I got to go, Miss Latham." Myree's eyes sought a pathway from the room.

"So soon? I thought we might have a chat."

Myree's gaze came guardedly to Diana's face. "About what?"

Diana's hand moved in an airy gesture. "Oh, this house for one thing."

"It's a fancy house made for high-heeled living, Miss Latham."

"Have you been here long?"

"Awhile."

"I'll bet you know more about it than most."

The old eyes lurked in shadowy sockets. "I reckon I could spill a few beans." The shriveled lips leered. "But I ain't going to."

Diana nodded. "I respect you for that, Myree."

The bony, harridan face drew away. "I reckon you're trying to pick me, Miss Latham. It ain't friendly to try and pick folks." The thin voice was tinged with sadness as if, for a moment, Myree had sensed a friend in Diana, a friend who had tried to use her.

Silently, Myree shuffled past Diana, pausing at the door. She turned, brooded on Diana for a moment. "Won't do you a whit of good to try and pick me, Miss Latham."

Diana took a halting step. "Myree, if you know anything that hasn't come to light . . ."

" 'Pears to me it's all come to light, Miss Latham. Seems plain that this is a house of sin and suffering." Myree's fingers curled about the ornate doorknob. "And if I was you, Miss Latham, I wouldn't try to rattle up the closeted skeletons in this place!"

Myree opened the door as if to punctuate the statement. Instantly, she fell back a step. Cloty was just outside, raising her knuckles to knock.

The two women gaped for a second. Cloty

raised her spectacles on their neck chain and stared. Myree slid past her with a cat-like movement.

Cloty came on into the room, closing the door, and making a small gesture with her head toward the hallway.

"She just brought some fresh towels," Diana explained. She looked at the closed door, listened for some sound in the silence beyond it. "Cloty," she said with a gusty sigh, "I'd swear that Myree could tell us a few things."

Cloty pursed her lips, lifted a forefinger to her temple, making a circular motion. "She might *imagine* that she could," Cloty said, "for the sake of her own sense of self-importance. Myree's an odd one, but she's strong and does her work well. And goodness knows you can't be choosey in finding help nowadays."

Cloty nervously fingered her dangling eyeglasses. Diana sensed a lot more on Cloty's mind than the subject of a domestic.

"What is it, Cloty?"

Cloty squinted at her narrowly. "Nurse Abernathy and I were just talking about you. She's quite put out with you."

"I'm sorry about that. I didn't mean to. . . ."

"No, no," Cloty interrupted. "That isn't important. She says you exhausted Lucy trying to communicate with some kind of fanciful code."

71

"We did communicate," Diana said.

Cloty grasped Diana's hand. Her excited strength caused Diana to wince.

"Finally! From Lucy herself!" Cloty's voice burst out. She gave Diana a small, unintentional shake. "Well? What did Lucy say?"

Diana disentangled her hand. "Not very much, I'm afraid. She warned me of danger in this house."

Cloty banged a hard little fist into her other palm. "That's quite enough!" She paced with quick, jerky steps. "That dear child, fearing for a friend even in her own suffering . . . You do see what it means, Diana?"

"I think I do. She was afraid that I would run a risk if I stayed here."

"Precisely! And if the tragedy she suffered was an accident, pure and simple, she'd have no reason to be afraid for you."

Diana eased to a boudoir chair and sank on the edge of it. "The same risk applies to anyone in this house, Cloty, who stumbles on a hint of the truth."

"Quite," Cloty said in her coolest governess voice. "The finger of death might well be poised for any unwitting soul who doesn't instantly recognize the hint that he or she stumbles upon."

The words seemed to hang. Diana shivered. Cloty detected the twitch through Diana's shoulders.

The old governess stood tall and querulous, looking down at the auburn sheen of Diana's crown.

"What will you do, my dear?" Without inflection, Cloty might have been asking what Diana would have for breakfast.

"Do?" Diana lifted her face. "Why, I'll stay."

Cloty patted her shoulder. "And I," she said, "will ease quietly into the village tomorrow—meaning that I'll bide my chance and slip away. And I shall have a talk with Constable Comage."

Cloty paused, fingering an earlobe, smiling a steely, mirthless smile. "I can predict the good constable's perfectly reasonable rejoinders. 'Miss Cloty,' he will say, 'the case is closed.' And I shall say, 'You will reopen it.' Then he'll say, squirming a little behind that beatup old desk, 'Miss Cloty, on what evidence? You have brought no new evidence. I have to have new evidence, Miss Cloty.' And I shall say, 'You will reopen it.' Finally, he'll recognize the futility of argument."

"I can believe that," Diana found a brief laugh. "But he and experts from New Orleans wrote it off as an accident after their investigation. What can your harried Constable Comage do that hasn't been done?"

"He can show up," Cloty said emphatically. "He can make motions. He can investigate. Don't forget, my dear, that only you and I know that he

73

has no new evidence. His act of reopening the case might in itself jar someone into giving us that hint we're so hungry for."

"Yes," Diana breathed, "someone feeling the strain of his crime, his secret."

Cloty drew a wispy linen handkerchief from the pocket of her dress and calmly wiped her palms. "Meanwhile, I suggest you retire, behind a locked door."

Diana rose, walking with Cloty across the room. There was a moment before Cloty left.

"Cloty . . ."

"Yes?"

"You've had your suspicions about Lucy's accident even before I came here."

"I have." Cloty nodded without hesitation.

"Why? On what basis?"

Cloty's forehead creased in a gradual frown. "Intuition, perhaps. An uncertainty about it being an accident because of the things I saw in Lucy's eyes . . . those dear eyes following me, trying desperately to tell me something. That's mainly what I have—the message of her eyes."

"Mainly?"

"Isn't that enough to make one wonder? To question? To suspect? One who has known a lifetime of closeness with Lucy, from the days of bedtime stories to the nightly horror of that room where she now is?"

"Yes, more than enough," Diana said.

"All right," Cloty grumped, "the other little thing will make you think I'm as cranky as poor Myree. So color me pixilated—but I won't believe that St. Joan would crash down upon the sweet child who was kneeling there in supplication!"

Chapter 5

Diana hovered restlessly in a thin veneer of sleep. Fragmentary, shadowy dreams beset her, wavering faces arising from swamp-like mists, towering statues reeling and crashing. She was alone in an abandoned, miles-long chapel, running in this direction and that, trying to call Lucy's name with a throat that would form no words. The slimy, moldy walls were rushing on her, burying her alive. She opened her mouth in a silent scream . . .

She lay gasping, seeing the flood of moonlight through her window. She was shivering, even though she was damp with perspiration. After a moment, she realized this wasn't a part of the dream. She had awakened.

Her breath abated, and she began to hold it in, listening to the silence, experiencing the feeling that something other than the dream had brought her to consciousness. Something in the real world. Here in the house. Or close-by outside. It wouldn't have taken much to pierce the shallow veil of troubled sleep.

Her eyes inched to the luminous hands of the small bedside clock. Almost three. Who could be up and about in this small morning hour? She must be mistaken. Probably the call of some bayou creature, a strange echo in her unaccustomed ears, had awakened her.

She pushed up a little from the cloying mass of her pillow and was about to punch it to a semblance of usual comfort when her hand froze in midair.

Her gaze flew to the door. And now she heard it without question, the thump-thump of footsteps. Passing her door. Moving on, as if they had halted briefly outside her room.

They were like the faint tap of a mallet on a muffled drum, steady, but uneven. Limping footsteps. Huxley Devereau's.

Diana's face drew to a hard frown. Where had the aging master of Devereau House gone at such an hour?

Then Diana realized, as the footsteps continued and faded to silence, that he wasn't coming in, but going out.

Wide awake now, the bed unpleasantly warm, she threw back the thin sheet and stood in her ankle-length gown.

77

Wafting curtains drew Diana to the open window and the coolness of the gentle breeze on her face. She stood with her hand propped on the window sill, content for a moment to draw the pleasant freshness into her lungs.

The blue-black sky was clotted here and there with buttermilk clouds that intensified the brightness of the full moon. Trees and fields stood out with sharp edges of shadow and silver-tinged clarity.

As she started to move from the window, Diana's angle of vision shifted, and she saw the car—and the woman—in the driveway below.

Diana was caught by the scene. The car and woman were the odd details completing the aspect of surrealism. The car was a small, foreign-made roadster with a white canvas top. The woman was straight and tall, regally tall. She wore a yellow turban and a multi-hued cloak that covered her from neck to wrists to ankles. Her features were shadowed, but Diana felt they would be handsomely chiseled.

The woman was simply standing there, waiting, moonlight drawing greens, yellows, and purples from the long straight lines of her dress. In her patient stillness she was like an idol carved by artistic, primitive hands.

A movement caught Diana's attention. She saw Huxley Devereau emerge from the shadows close by the house. His limping gait carried him straight to the woman and her small car.

The woman made no move as Huxley reached her side. They were of a height, moonlight burnishing her turban and his bare head to crowns of gold and silver.

"Domina," he spoke the woman's name with quiet respect and affection, "thank you for coming."

"I am always near when your spirit is anguished, Huxley." The phrases weren't at all stilted, coming from Domina's lips. Diana had never heard such a softly rich contralto. The accent was liquidly Cajun. It was a voice, Diana thought, made for spirituals—or incantations to ward off demons.

"I didn't want to call you at such an hour," the old man was saying, "but it was the final hour I could take of being alone."

"Then it was the proper hour," Domina said. "Did the arrival of the stranger, the young woman, have anything to do with it?"

"Inadvertently," Huxley said heavily. "I wanted her to visit. I believed she would be good for Lucy. But she has been to the chapel ruins with Tony. She has managed to communicate with Lucy. She has suspicions, Domina."

"Groundless suspicions, my old friend," Domina intoned. "The reactions of a mind, steeped with friendship, jarred by sudden reality."

Huxley searched the shadowed face, needing reassurance and strength.

"But if not," he said heavily, "it opens up the chance that Lucy is suffering by design . . . for the sins and blights of Devereau House . . ."

His words broke with a racking groan. A sob shook through him. The tall figure beside him moved at last, raising an arm and drawing him to her. His face fell on her shoulder. He uttered a thick sound of despair.

"You mustn't think in these channels," Domina said, a sharpness in her husky voice. "Little wonder that the lonely hours have become unendurable. Come now, we will go and talk the problem out. The morning will bring the sun, as it did before our advent, as it will for a million years after we are gone."

Her presence, the sound of her voice seemed medicinal for the old patrician. He lifted his head, drawing back and standing a little straighter.

"Why do you put up with me, Domina?"

"Because I'm your friend. Because you put up with me when I need you. Because there are no secrets, no unspoken ranklings between us."

She offered her hand. Huxley took it, and they stood a moment.

"The rarest thing on this earth," she said, "is true and honest friendship between a man and a woman. We have that, Huxley, untainted by carnality. We are utterly free of duplicity because our relationship is of the spirit. Is it not a treasure?"

"Above all material values," Huxley said. Lifting her hand a little he escorted her around the car with a courtly graciousness, opened the door for her, helped her into the small bucket seat.

When he'd settled himself under the steering wheel, he started the car and idled the engine quietly. He backed slowly without turning on the headlights.

Diana leaned out and saw the lights flare when the car was well away from the house. The soft purr of the engine soon faded.

Settled again in bed, Diana mused on the scene she'd witnessed. Who was Domina? What was the secret anguish that worked in Huxley Devereau?

The strangeness of the meeting gave it the quality of the fitful, episodic dreams that had preceded it this night.

Diana turned, chunked her pillow. She thought she would never sleep, but unaccountably her eyes were opening at last, and the light at the window was sun brightness instead of moon haze.

Her first thought of the day was of Lucy, and when she came out of her room wearing casual cotton blouse and skirt, she hurried along the gallery to Lucy's door.

The stalwart, green-starched form of Nurse Abernathy responded to Diana's soft knock.

"Good morning." Diana tried to see past the blockading figure. "How is Lucy today?"

"Asleep. Resting quite well—after the excitation of yesterday's reunion."

That was that. Clearly, the robot, the medical automaton, would decide when the patient was up to visitation.

Abernathy's big-boned face remained an expressionless mask of sandstone, but her hazel eyes relented slightly. "Please understand, Miss Latham, I'm not trying to be difficult. My concern is what the charts, gauges, and dials tell me about the condition of the patient."

"I'm grateful for that," Diana parried. "The first excitement of seeing me, of knowing that I'm here, is over for Lucy now. Visits from now on won't have that element of stress. So if you don't mind, I'll come back when she's awake."

"Come as often as you like," the nurse said, her tone making no promises that the door would be opened when Diana came.

With a nod of dismissal, Abernathy closed the door, leaving Diana to stare at the wooden barrier with a sudden flush of angry pink in her cheeks.

She had no recourse but to turn and go away. Could the nurse be right? Was she, Diana, the worst emotional medicine for Lucy?

No, Diana thought as she hurried down the broad stairway, I won't believe that for a minute.

If the positions were reversed, Lucy's presence would be a tonic I'd need.

What then of Abernathy, the nurse in charge? Was she just a pig-headed machine who would go by the book even if a patient were gasping his last? Or did she have reasons of her own for wanting to keep Diana away?

Wrapped in her thoughts, Diana almost bumped into Tony as he stepped from the dining room into the grand hall.

"Wups!" Tony sidestepped. "We're off like a jet this morning."

"Oh, hi, Tony." Diana glanced at the small, indistinct mottle of yellow on his forehead. "How's the bean that Ozar Fant tried to crack?"

"I'm immune to slings, arrows, and brainings," he said, bending slightly to peer at her. "But you're a bit on the wan side, chick. Ghosts of Devereau House keep you awake rattling their chains?"

"The only chains visible around here are the velvet kind," she laughed. "Now will you lead on to the kitchen? I'll burn my own egg this morning, I'm so late coming down."

"Cook would never hear of it, and neither would I. You take yourself out to the patio and seat yourself under one of those umbrellas, and I'll join you presently."

He was as good as his word, wheeling a small

serving cart alongside the metal table where Diana sat.

With a waiter-like bow, he uncovered serving dishes. "Appetizer of papaya juice, m'am, scrambled eggs, country ham two years in the aging, grits—we never omit grits, redeye gravy, hot biscuits, and your choice of jams and marmalades. Have to, m'am."

His mood of boyish humor was infectious. The morning was beautiful, with a deep blue sky and the scent of flowers drifting across the patio. It was a hint of the idyllic moments that Devereau House had once offered.

Tony had poured a second cup of coffee for himself, slouching in the nearest chair to Diana, looking out over the pool. His attire was less belligerently Cajun this morning, still the knit shirt and jeans, but not leftovers from a rummage sale. The shaggiest ends of his dark hair had been razor-touched by a barber in the village late yesterday or early this morning.

Lowering his coffee cup, he broke his musings. "How'd it go last night?"

"How should it have gone? Robin was very nice . . ."

"Robin," he said, turning his head to look at her, "is the little golden hourglass they paint on black widow spiders."

"Really now, Tony!"

"And Philip? I guess he was the epitome of the

84

clean-cut Establishment man, the backbone of our country."

Diana felt her cheeks tinge with color.

"Hmmm," Tony said. "I note a reaction. But don't get ideas about Philip Lockridge, my pet, or Robin will choose a nicely dulled knife."

Why do I want to reach and take your hand even when you needle me, Tony, Diana wondered. She nibbled a piece of buttery biscuit. Her eyes teased. "I'm not scared of dulled knives, Tony, if I want something bad enough."

His reflex wasn't what she'd expected. A tiredness veiled his eyes. He looked away, picking up his coffee, looking out over the swampy distances. Then his finely cut profile hardened, losing its boyish vulnerability.

"He runs hard, Diana. But don't let him ride with your colors. Because he won't win."

"Win what, Tony?"

"His game. His Jacob to my Esau." He turned enough to give her a sidelong look. "Remember the Biblical story, Diana? The birthright was Esau's, but he liked to hunt and wander the hills and fields and look at the natural, growing things. Meanwhile, Jacob stayed close to the old man, their father, and plotted to take the birthright."

"I know," Diana murmured, "I'm familiar with the story."

"This time the ending will be different."

"Will it, Tony?"

85

"What's that supposed to mean?"

She concentrated on the hard-cured country ham with knife and fork. "Nothing, Tony. It's really none of my business."

He stirred, tautly. "No? Then I'm asking for your opinion."

"All right," she said, "since you insist." She met his eyes. "Last night you gave them the field. How can you win if you run away from the clinches?"

She expected a glower, or a hurt look of rebuff. But not the sudden smile that parted his lips. "Did it look like that?"

"What else?"

"Maybe I ducked out to get a haircut—or to keep your dinner meeting pleasant." His smile faded. A shadow brooded across his lean face. "Or you could be right. Maybe the old subconscious would like to tack a shack together on a swamp hummock and do the Thoreau bit."

"What would that solve, Tony?"

"It would bequeath to Philip the rot that lurks behind the facade of ye olde mansion," he said grimly.

"But I think you would take a part of Devereau House to that hermit's shack, Tony."

His shoulders lifted, fell. "Could be. But you could escape, Diana, before you become too involved."

"Trying to run me off, Tony? Don't you like having me here?"

"From a purely selfish point of view, I'd like to keep you around for a long time to come."

"That's nice. I'd hate to think of myself as a guest on sufferance."

"Never that, Diana." He slouched back in his chair, his dark eyes brooding on her. "You are some chick, and if I let myself, I could fall in love with you."

She was warmed, and a small breath caught. "After knowing me only a day?" she asked lightly.

"Why not? How much time does it take? Anyway, I've known you for quite awhile. From the day Lucy came home with her talk and all her memories of you. She brought the image of you to this house, you know." His lips tugged in a crooked grin. "But I didn't say I had let myself, did I?"

"You can turn love on or off, just like that?"

"Keep it at arm's length, at least," he said. "You open up to love, you risk getting hurt, deep down, where it counts."

Diana felt hushed. It must have taken something very painful for him to want to put his heart under lock and key. It must have happened a long time ago, when he was childishly open to hurt.

In a flash of intuition, she wondered if it had to do with his mother and her suicidal race one macabre night to an untimely death . . .

Diana continued the casual motions of breakfast. "Yes, Tony, there are risks. But without them, how do you find the joys of love?"

"You mean the illusions? Who says I need them?"

Before she could answer, he lifted a palm and turned the conversation with a quick grin. "Truce! Let's not grim up such a beautiful day."

He was standing up as he spoke. "Dad wants to talk to me this morning. I think it's about the merger of Nectar Sugar and Devereau raw materials that Robin is so keenly after. Shouldn't take long. Later, we should think up something more enjoyable for the first day of your vacation than crossing verbal swords."

"Okay, Tony," Diana laughed. "Truce." She watched him stride from the patio and returned to her breakfast with a bemused shake of her head.

She was finishing her coffee when voices from the playroom drifted to her.

"Good morning, Myree," Philip Lockridge's hearty voice intoned. "Always busy with the elbow grease and furniture polish."

"Plenty to keep a-body busy," the gray-topnotted menial responded.

"Miss Latham around?"

"Right there on the patio, sir, having her breakfast."

"Yes, I see her now. Thank you, Myree."

Diana turned and saw Philip emerging from the playroom. In slacks and knitted shirt, he was a wide-shouldered, cleanly-hewn figure, a smile lighting his vigorous good looks as he crossed to the table.

"Good morning, Diana. I see they've initiated you to our Louisiana breakfasts."

"I won't care for a bite of lunch," Diana laughed.

He sat down in the chair Tony had vacated. The comparison struck Diana. There was no looseness, slouching, indolence, boyish uncertainty in the chair's present occupant.

Philip folded his hands on the table, the sunlight catching the college ring he wore. "This is usually my week-day golf date, but I phoned the club and told the others to find a substitute fourth. I had a far more interesting prospect. I hope you haven't already planned your day."

"Not yet."

"Good. Like to ride? Horses, I mean?"

Diana dropped her napkin beside her plate. "Kansas farm girl, remember? I don't ride prettily, but I can hang on like a Texas wrangler."

"Then how about we see some Devereau countryside?"

"Give me about five minutes to change into some slacks."

Philip courteously rose as she sprang to her feet. She hurried inside, aware of his steady eyes following her movements.

He was finishing a cup of coffee when Diana

reappeared on the patio. She had donned dark blue slacks, a comfortable white blouse, sturdy shoes, and tied her hair in a ponytail with a folded scarf.

Face lighted with quiet appreciation, he took her hand and they set off toward the distant riding ring, barn, and stables.

The sun was warm, the breeze soft, and insects hummed a whispering paean over the verdant fields. With Philip moving easily beside her, Diana felt as if the shadows of Devereau House were falling far behind.

"Huxley has a pinto that should be perfect for a western riding she-male," Philip suggested waggishly.

The shadow of the huge barn flowed over them, Philip pausing. He looked about. Off to the left was the riding ring. Some distance away in the other direction stood the stables, a short row of individual stalls, to or three with horses visible over the chest-high gates.

"Don't see the groom around," Philip said, "or anyone else for that matter. Back in a minute. If I don't find him, we'll saddle our own."

Diana watched him walk away. Aside from Lucy, she thought, Philip is the dependable, predictable one. Philip was the strength of a steady river current, while the others were rapids, whirlpools, backwash ponds.

She saw him disappear beyond the stables. She

remembered a small, weatherbeaten cottage in a grove of trees not far from the stables. It was probably where the groom lived.

She idled back and forth in front of the towering barn. It was much cooler here in the shade, and the breeze had the faintest taint of bayou lushness and decay.

Later, she was to wonder what caused her to stop and look up. A soft rustling in the barnloft . . . the hint of a sound that didn't quite belong . . .

Her eyes froze the scene. The high gable of the barn cut the blueness of the sky in a broken angle. Below the gable yawned the darkly blank haymow, the opening through which hay and fodder were conveyored to the barnloft. And spearing down from the haymow was a long-handled pitchfork, needle-sharp tines plunging at Diana's face.

Chapter 6

She didn't know she had moved, until her feet entangled and her shoulder jarred against the ground.

She glimpsed the flash of the tines inches away, heard their sibilant bite as they implanted the pitchfork with a long handle quivering.

She was faint, almost retchingly ill. But thought of a second attack brought her scrambling to her feet.

Stumbling back, she looked wildly at the hay-mow. Her gasping breath matched the furious pounding of her heart.

Nothing moved up there. No sound broke the stillness. She slipped a glance aside, but didn't see Philip.

As the storm of panic eased, she took a couple of halting steps, drawn by the hypnotic sight of the pitchfork handle standing so perfectly upright from the earth.

She touched the shaft, and it was slick, polished by many hours of laboring hands. Slowly, she slipped the tines free. Their long thin sharpness was undulled by the few clinging crumbs of dirt.

Her skin prickled from the thought of what those tines might have done to her. And the thought stirred an eddy of anger, a sense of violation, a kindling of outrage.

Her lips compressed, and her face slowly lost the pallor of panic. She looked once more, fruitlessly, for Philip, and eased toward the barn, holding the pitchfork with both hands.

The shadow of the broad, open doorway flowed over her. Every nerve rawly alert, she scanned the twilight-dim interior. It was a cow barn. She could see placid bovines chewing their cuds in a couple of the stalls on either side of the wide, uncluttered trot area. There was no sign of other life, except for a bluebottle fly that came to buzz her quizzically.

She inched along, keeping to the middle of the open trot, her eyes stabbing every shadow. She stopped at the further end of the trot, beside the ladder that reached up and disappeared into the barn loft. Her taut stare searched the rectangular entry through the floor of the hayloft high above. It was like a patch of dark gray fog, undisturbed, as silent as the mouth of a tomb.

93

She ached with the urge to prod the inhuman pitchfork-thrower into the open, to make him show his face. But her common sense took stronger control. Better wait for Philip. Better still, go and find him.

She backed away, watching the ladder. When she felt the open space of the doorway at her back, she was aware of the weight of the pitchfork still in her hands. She propped it beside the heavy upright timber of the jamb and fled into the sunlight.

Philip was still nowhere to be seen, and Diana ran toward the stables. As she reached the end of the stalls, she saw him finally, striding across the strip of open field that separated the stables from the groom's cottage.

Her burst of speed caught him up short. A quick frown creased his forehead. He caught her arm above the elbow as she practically fell against him.

"Diana! What is it?"

Now that he was near, a whipleather strength to borrow from, a reactive shiver shot through her. "Philip . . . in the hayloft . . . someone tried to drop a pitchfork on me."

He stared at her, speechless.

"Hurry, Philip! He'll get away, lose himself in the thickets and swamps."

"Diana . . ." Then with eyes riveted on her

face, he decided that questions could wait until later.

Somehow, she matched his pace, and they reached the barn side by side.

"Philip . . . please be careful . . . Here, wait . . . the pitchfork." She turned from the door-jamb, holding the tool out to him.

He took it, hefted it without visible signs of fear, though his eyes were several shades darker. With a final flick of his gaze across her face, he turned and whipped away, gripping the pitchfork like a lance, a no-nonsense defensive weapon.

At the hayloft ladder, he paused to shift his grip, the tines lifting, biting into the upper twilight ahead of him as he mounted rung by rung.

Diana stood dry-throated, little twitches catching at her muscles here and there. She heard the soft thud of his footsteps, the rustling of hay. Her head moved slowly while her straining ears followed his progress through the hayloft. He worked his way to the front. Now he was crossing over, cautiously returning.

She ran to the ladder when his descending feet appeared, stepping aside as he dropped the last few feet.

He propped the pitchfork against the ladder, and slipped a handkerchief from his pocket. He mashed it against his palms and swabbed it over the glisten of sweat on his chiseled cheeks and forehead. A tension-easing breath slipped from him. "Nothing up there but several tons of hay, Diana."

"Then he got away while I was looking for you!"

He slipped an arm about her shoulders, keeping her close to his side while he walked her from the barn. "Now tell me what happened, Diana."

"I've told you, Philip. I was waiting for you, in the shadow of the barn. I heard a small noise, looked up, and the pitchfork was falling at me."

"But why, Daina? You're a stranger. We all wanted you here, welcomed you here."

"Why? Because of Lucy!"

"I'm afraid I don't understand."

In the open portal, she pulled away, turning to face him. Calmly, she told him about the way she and Lucy had communicated, how Lucy had warned her.

"Don't you see, Philip, it means that someone is afraid Lucy told me more than she really did, gave me a clue to what actually happened to her."

Philip gave it hard thought for a moment, rubbing the back of his neck.

"Diana . . ." his voice was an unwilling effort, "the pitchfork was inside the barn, propped innocently beside the doorway."

"I carried it in there, Philip. I . . . Here . . . I'll show you . . . where the pitchfork struck. It left holes in the ground when I pulled it . . ."

She had turned, pointing. Her voice trailed off. The marks were gone. The marks of the tines had been smoothed over.

She tried to swallow. Anxiously, she scanned a wider area. She looked up at the haymow and her eyes followed the remembered flight of the pitchfork until she was again staring at the ground.

Her face crept up, woebegone. "Please believe me, Philip. The thing really did try to skewer me."

With a gentle smile, he drew her to him, touching her head, resting her cheek against his shoulder.

"Poor, dear Diana. It's been a lousy start for a vacation."

"You must believe me, Philip," she said, her voice muffled against him. "I didn't imagine the pitchfork!"

"But it doesn't mean that someone threw it at you, Diana. That hay packed in the loft makes a surface as slick as ice. Isn't it possible someone left the tool carelessly after forking down hay? If it began inching forward under its own weight, it was bound to fall from the haymow."

Diana stepped back, a wash of color in her cheeks. "Just a harmless quirk of natural forces? Can you honestly believe in such a coincidence?"

"If I'm to believe at all that the pitchfork fell . . ."

"Then believe—or disbelieve—anything you like, Philip!"

She wheeled about and started away. She'd moved only a few steps when Philip was beside her, his touch on her arm restraining her.

"Take it easy, m'am." His drawl was exaggerated, a parry. "You-all has some yankee temper, sho'nuff!"

She stood, relenting, unable to combat the gentle chiding of his eyes.

He reached and brushed a small stray wisp of hair from her ear, his fingertip lingering. "Let's give this whole bit a thought. Who, besides me, knows about this danger signal you've had from Lucy?"

"I told Tony, and Cloty. And Nurse Abernathy knows."

"We can dismiss the nurse. She wasn't aware of Lucy's existence until a considerable time after the accident. That leaves Tony and Cloty. Do you think either of them would topple a stone statue onto Lucy and, today, shag out here while you were putting on something for riding, lay in wait, ambush you from the hayloft?"

Philip dropped his hand to his side, waiting for her answer.

"It does sound really flipped out, when you put it that way," Diana admitted.

"You're the same lovely image with intestinal fortitude to take Iaxtaca in stride, Diana. But seeing Lucy yesterday was a hundred times worse than the grimmest shock that Iaxtaca had to offer."

"Philip, I am not. . . ."

He laid a finger tenderly across her lips. "Give me a chance, will you? Let me help. You've the strength to be objective about the whole thing."

She pulled away and stood stonily. "All right, I'm as objective as a researcher on the big end of a microscope. Where would you like to start, Philip?"

Her tone needled him a little, but his eyes were understanding and patient.

"Start with Lucy," he said. "Nerves shattered. Helpless. Neural circuits out of kilter. Nothing to do but lay there and think . . . and after awhile it begins to seem impossible that her beloved St. Joan could have done such a horrible thing. Surely, some earthly hand was involved."

"And paranoia has shown its ugly face?"

Philip's jaw muscles bunched tiredly. "Don't you know I'd give my right arm, Diana . . . But could Lucy have suffered such an accident to her central nervous system without it affecting her mind?"

He broke off, etchings of pain creeping through his face. But any sympathy Diana felt was lost in her fear of what he was saying. Of what might well be the truth. Her mind writhed ahead, anticipating his next statement.

"And you, dearest Diana . . ." he had to take a breath, "as if the shock of seeing Lucy wasn't enough, add the final horror of her weird warning . . . It's only natural that you'd be jumpy. You wouldn't be human otherwise."

His assessment was uncomfortably close to the state of her nerves. Without actually wanting to hurt him, she had to strike back. "And now we have two paranoids!"

His nostrils flared with a hint of exasperation. "I didn't say that, Diana—and you know darn well I didn't! Anyone conditioned by the heartbreaking sight of Lucy and the frightfulness of her warning would have jumped to the conclusion that the pitchfork had been thrown deliberately."

He thumbed a rivulet of perspiration from his cheek, and it was his turn to fire back defensively. "Purely human reaction. Unless you're a rock-nerved exception to the human race?"

The question snapped the separation to which the chain of talk had led. Diana found herself laughing at the blunt look on his face.

"You're a pragmatist, Philip."

"I try," he said, "to line up the concrete facts I have at hand."

And you've nothing concrete to prove the pitchfork really fell at all, Diana thought.

Yet she didn't feel critical or resentful. He'd accepted her word that the pitchfork had come slipping from the loft. He probably wasn't convinced that it had threatened her or gnashed its tines into the spot where she'd have been standing, if she hadn't looked up.

But she knew intuitively that he was reserving judgment. He would be more watchful for her sake. And that was a part of his strength.

She liked this quietly balanced part of him, and felt a little more secure.

"Saddles and horses are concrete facts," she reminded, "even if grooms aren't around."

"I guess he's working with the colts over in the pasture," Philip said. He bunched his lips for an instant. "You sure you want to go ahead with the ride?"

"Why not? What could I tell your Constable Comage, or show to a detective from New Orleans? What more could we do here?"

His eyes enlivened; a smile warmed his lips. "Know something? Lucy used every superlative in the book describing you—and still sold you short."

An hour later Diana drew her pinto up for a breather on the shore of a small, crystalline-blue lake ringed with wild palms. Philip reined his dun-colored gelding beside her. His animal pawed a forehoof and shook the bridle at the smell of water.

"It's good water," he said. "We'll let them drink."

They dismounted and led their horses to the

water's edge. While the animals dipped their muzzles, Diana stood stroking the pinto's withers, watching to see that he didn't gorge the water too freely.

The past hour had been a good one, with fresh, clean air in her face and good hard physical activity to sweep the dross from her mind.

It was her first chance to see the countryside in detail, and she and Philip had covered a good part of it. Compared to the barrenness of a Kansas farm and the poverty of Iaxtaca, the land had an aspect of Eden. Things grew here as if the earth had a wild joy in giving forth verdant life.

The pines towered, bursting with resinous vigor; the sugar cane fields were so lushly grown a person could lose herself ten feet away in the endless green masses; startled rabbits had flipped saucy cottontails when the pinto had distanced the dun across a field of swaying broomsage; water oaks had softly rustled a welcome; and a giant banyan tree had offered shade, its ten thousand roots trailing from gnarled limbs to earth to form among themselves a miniature forest; even the air was imbued with life, feeding festoons and veils of Spanish moss that wafted on hoary cypresses whose rock-like trunks were splashed with the color of parasitic, wild orchids.

Little creatures seemed to be everywhere, peering, rustling, darting across a bridle path. There

102

were showers of birds, and a bushy-tailed squirrel fussing from a tree limb at their passage.

"That's about enough, fellow." Diana reined the pinto back from the water. He swung his head to give her a mischievous look. She patted his muzzle. He was a horse to her liking, frisky but not capricious, taking a joy in stretching out his legs. "You could almost turn me into a horse thief, boy," she laughed, as she toed the stirrup and mounted.

Philip swung into the saddle. "Tired?"

Diana shook her head. "I could go on all day, but these fellows burn oats, not gasoline."

"Yes, I suppose we had better be getting back," Philip agreed regretfully. "There's a boondock gravelled road not far from here. You'll see it in a minute."

They veered the horses, walking them alongside a wall of wild, thorny thicket. When the brambles fell behind, an arm of the lake curved into view that Diana hadn't seen before, a serene and lovely lagoon sheltered by tall palms and willows.

Across the stretch of water in a shaded glen on the further shore stood a picturesque cottage. It was low and rambling with sapling-railed porches. It stood out with bold red paint, narrow white shutters snugging its windows. But it was not the sight of the cottage or the white wooden pier where a small sailing boat bobbed that caused

Diana to halt the pinto. Rather, it was the view of the small car parked near the house. Small and foreign, with a white canvas top.

Unless a lot of people around here owned such a car, Diana thought, I'm looking at the little job that carried Huxley away from Devereau House in the wee hours.

"Philip, who lives over there?"

The dun, sensing most of the ride was over, champed at the bit. Philip controlled the animal with a touch of knee and rein. "A woman known as Domina. Why?"

"No particular reason—but I thought that would be her place."

Philip curbed the restlessness of his horse with the automatic reflexes of an experienced horseman.

"Lucy didn't spare the Devereau details during the long months in Iaxtaca, did she?"

"Lucy didn't open closets on family skeletons, if that's what you mean, Philip. I happened to see Huxley and Domina drive away from the house early this morning."

"Then I should explain the situation. It smacks of the weird, and you'll see why we don't talk about it." Philip threw a grim look at the brick-red cottage. "She plays the role of benevolent sorceress to the troubled old king. Like the witches of Macbeth, or the occult seeress to whom the Biblical King Saul brought his tormented soul."

He slackened the rein on the fidgeting, side-stepping dun. "We might as well ride over and say a polite hello. Huxley and Domina have come onto the porch, and no doubt spotted us."

Chapter 7

"So you are the guest at Devereau House." Domina responded with a gracious smile to the introduction which Huxley Devereau had just made.

Domina and Huxley had come around from the lake side of the cottage when Diana and Philip had ridden up and hitched the horses at the white picket fence alongside the crude, back-parish road.

As a group, the four now strolled inside the cottage, chatting ice-breaking inanities, Domina remarking that it was a good day for riding and Philip joking that Diana was really a rider with a wild-west show and not a school teacher at all.

Domina, Diana instantly decided, was even more striking than she'd seemed last night. She was tall and regal in a garment of rustling white that flowed to her sandaled feet. Framed in jet-black page boy and bangs, her pale olive face with its strong features and large, shadowed eyes had a rare mystique. If time-warping miracles were possible, Domina might have stepped from an ancient Egyptian temple and a priestess ritual to the goddess Isis to appear in the hushed sultriness of the bayou countryside.

Huxley was ushering them in with a happy show of welcome, but Diana wondered if the old man resented the intrusion.

Domina suggested a tall, cooling drink after their ride and excused herself.

Diana and Philip sat on the white sailcloth couch, while Huxley chose the matching chair nearby.

The living room, Diana thought, was hardly the dank abode of Philip's sorceress. It was a charming room of bright gay colors, from the pale green shag rug to bleached wood paneling. Several excellent bayou landscapes in oil and charcoal sketches graced the walls, and exquisite little hand-carved figurines sparingly peopled the tables.

Domina appeared with a silver tray bearing tall, frosty glasses of pink punch decorated with green sprigs of fresh mint.

Philip's talk drifted to a dryness in the cane fields that had missed Diana's eyes, and he and Huxley were soon discussing the qualities of sugar cane.

"One man by himself thinks of business," Domina remarked to Diana. "Two men invaribly get around to talking it."

Philip turned from Huxley with an apology, but Domina shushed him with a lifted finger. "Please continue. It will give me a chance to show Diana around—if she'd care to see the place."

"I'd love to."

Domina led the way through a small dining room and compact kitchen. She and Diana emerged on the long porch overlooking the lake.

"It's a simple life out here," Domina said. "I imagine it would be maddeningly boring to most. But I have my flower garden. My painting—I like to set up an easel under that weeping willow. The skiff you see there at the pier, when I'm in the mood to unfurl the sail and coast the quiet of the lagoon. And people. I have my people."

Her gaze drifted across the reaches of swamp and jungle. "Out there is their fortress, Diana, a redoubt where life hasn't changed for generations. The home of the true Cajuns, with their language, their customs of old Acadia mingled with the superstitions of black Africans running away from slavery."

Domina half-seated herself on the sapling porch rail, leaning against the upright hewn support. Her head turned with swan-like movement. "You seem to have recognized me out there in the yard, Diana."

"I saw you last night," Diana said with a hint of

embarrassment, "when you met Huxley and drove away."

"You needn't feel uncomfortable about it," Domina smiled. "Huxley and I have never hidden our friendship. Neither do we parade it, for very simple reasons. Few people could understand it or let us have it for what it is. It's a friendship wholly of the spirit. Can you comprehend?"

"I think so."

"When Devereau House becomes too much, Huxley can find a comfort in the simplistic surroundings of the cottage. Out here, no questions are asked. There is no guilt, no remorse, no tormenting past. Just the quiet and peace of the ever-present now."

Diana felt the magnetic, hypnotic aura of the woman, almost like a tangible mist. Lesser figures, Diana thought, have taken the role of guru, established cults.

Domina had called the bayou people her people in a real sense. Easily, Diana could imagine the part the cottage played in lives tainted with the superstitions of old Africa. A temple, for all its casual charm, complete with high priestess.

"Do they come here often—your people?"

"When their souls despair," Domina said.

Diana leaned her hands on the porch railing, looking at the lake. If through her powers of hypnotic suggestion Domina could offer temporary relief, was it so wrong?

Yes, Diana thought, it's wrong, because Domina should use her gifts to lead her people to truth instead of reinforcing dark uncertainties and superstitions.

"Don't judge me too harshly, my dear."

Diana glanced about quickly. Domina was smiling. Her large, limpid eyes reflected a gentle forgiveness for another's doubts and disbeliefs.

A pulse crept through Diana's throat, and she needed strength to break the hold of Domina's eyes. Certainly she can't tune in my thoughts, Diana told herself firmly, it's just that she has an uncanny knack for catching and interpreting every hint that steals unknowingly through the other person's face.

"Are those your oils and sketches in the living room?" Diana asked, turning the conversation to neutral ground.

"Yes."

"They're lovely."

"I have many others. Would you like to see them?"

"Very much."

The northern portion of the cottage was a huge, rambling studio. Entering with Domina from the end of the porch, Diana had an impression of clutter and disarray common to most indefatigable artists. Portraits and landscapes were hung, stacked, propped against the walls. Paint-splotched tables were crowded with brush pots, crumpled pigment tubes, canvas trimmings. Stained with every hue of the rainbow, a couple of old smocks hung on nails beside the doorway. In the middle of the room stood an easel holding a nearly finished view of the lagoon.

"I can see you're surprised by their numbers," Domina said.

"There must be scores, even hundreds, of them!"

"A lifetime's work," Domina laughed. "And I won't tell you how long a lifetime."

Diana was drawn to the portraits that filled the inner wall. There were several of Huxley Devereau, spanning a period of years. Diana was instantly engrossed. Here was a Huxley with the parchment skin smoothed and invigorated, the chin proudly firm, the cheeks smooth and lean, the eyes flashing. A crown prince.

"He was a young man of much fire and many gifts," Domina said. "If he had a weakness, it was a lack of self-discipline. Perhaps he needed challenges, and Devereau House offered none."

Close by, a picture drew Diana's eyes slowly from the young Huxley. It was the portrait of a pixie girl, dark hair careless and wind-blown about her face. Her cheap, wanton prettiness, Diana mused, would have lasted barely past the moment of its blooming; then the lurking avidity, the greed and discontent, would have eroded the face.

"Was she really like that?" Diana asked.

"Many, many years ago she was."

"Then you did a marvelous piece of work. I can sense an unwholesome future in her face—and I feel a little sorry for her."

"It was one of my best paintings, and earliest," Domina said at Diana's shoulder. "I was fascinated by what I saw in the face. Not in the flesh and bone. In the real face."

"Who was she?"

"Just a girl," Domina said. "A Cajun girl who hated a shanty on stilts and labors in the yam patch. Her name was Prospera Clantell."

"Prospera," Diana said. "A lovely name."

"But a mis-nomer, I'm afraid," Domina smiled. "She was born to poverty and left Acadia a life-time ago."

Diana moved on slowly, gaining new insight into Cajun country with each painting. These were faces of a reckless, proud, fiery breed.

As Diana turned, a fresh portrait on the floor, propped against the wall caught her up short. The twisted, misshapen old face leaped at her, from canvas still unframed.

She bent, staring. "Ozar Fant!" And a residue of fright stirred in her as the remembered the gaunt old man charging around the chapel after he had clubbed Tony. Yet in the painting, Fant wasn't frightful at all. Domina had given the awry

112

eyes a quality of suffering and compassion. They peered humbly from the gargoyle visage, not seeking pity but offering it.

Remembering the old man with that chunk of tree limb, the painting seemed a travesty.

"Yes, do you know him?" Domina was asking.

"I saw him once, briefly," Diana said. "Tony Devereau told me who he was."

"A harmless old soul," Domina said. "He took squatter's right on a bayou shack and lives from hand to mouth. I've had him do some yard work. One day I saw him returning a nestling to its mother, very gently and with great care as he set a ladder and climbed up the tree to the nest. He didn't know I was watching from the house, and it was that moment when I decided to paint him."

And if you'd seen him clubbing Tony, Diana thought, you'd have done a different job on the eyes . . .

"Would you stay and eat?" Domina changed the subject.

"It's kind of you," Diana said as they strolled from the studio, "but perhaps Philip and I should be getting back."

They walked along the porch, and as they were about to re-enter the house, Domina paused. "Please come back, any time. I know that your first view of me—meeting Huxley outside the house and all—wasn't the best of impressions. But

113

appearances do sometimes deceive. Huxley and I met quietly outside the house simply because we didn't want to disturb anyone at such an hour."

"You don't owe me an explanation."

"Of course I don't. But Lucy loves you like a sister, and Huxley is very fond of you. In a real sense, you are a part of Devereau House, and I want us to be friends."

"I can't see any reason why we shouldn't be."

"Good." Domina tilted her handsome head, scrutinizing Diana. "Before your vacation is over, I'd like to paint you."

Diana grinned. "What hinted qualities would the canvas reveal?"

"You'll have to wait and see for yourself," Domina bantered. "But it will be an interesting portrait, because there is character in the face."

Domina opened the door, but refrained a moment longer from moving inside. "By the way, Diana, don't be afraid of me. I help my people, true. Sometimes with ageless remedies that science is just now discovering in the African bush. Sometimes as an amateur psychiatrist—and a first-rate one, speaking without false modesty. But," she added, a twinkle, subtly wise and gently chiding, in her eyes, "I'm hardly a practitioner of the arts of voodoo."

The impression of the strange woman lingered with Diana during the return ride to Devereau House.

She and Philip dismounted at the stables and loosened saddle cinches.

"I'm famished," he remarked.

Her silence brought his glance. "Ride frazzle you? I didn't mean to overdo it on your first day, Diana."

"Oh, no," she said, "the ride was relaxing. I needed to get out and move. I was just thinking of Domina."

"Quite a personality."

"She is that," Diana nodded. "What does she do, Philip?"

"Do?" He swung both saddles onto his shoulders, grasping one with either hand. "I guess you could say she just follows her life style. She could pick any she wants."

"She's wealthy?"

"She could trade in those little foreign roadsters every time the tops get dirty," he laughed, humping toward the tack room. "She had a grandfather who owned a few acres of apparently worthless scrub land—smack in the middle of what turned out to be a Louisiana oil reserve."

They snacked a belated lunch from the refrigerators in the huge old kitchen and were stacking the few dishes they'd used when Robin Toutain came in. Diana saw Robin framed in the doorway before Philip did. She saw the raw fire in Robin's eyes, quickly masked by Robin's smile for Philip.

"Have a good ride?" Robin asked pleasantly.

She was a lovely image of cream and gold, crossing the red brick floor of the kitchen. She was wearing a chic double-knit suit of blue piped in yellow to match her hair. A slender attache case was tucked under her arm.

"Wonderful," Philip said. "Diana's now native to our countryside."

"That sounds cozy." Robin laid the thin briefcase on the heavy, age-mellowed kitchen table. She faced Philip with a small sigh. "Sorry to be a wet blanket, darling, but we do have a problem. Quavely called from Houston about the machinery for the refinery addition. Seems they've run into a supply hangup."

"I'm not surprised," Philip said, "Quavely was bound to run into shortages with that foundry strike going on."

"And each day that deliveries are delayed means an idle day for our own construction crew. We can't very well afford that." While she was speaking Robin fetched a few sheets of annotated paper from the attache case.

"I've already listed several alternate suppliers," she said, "and estimated differences in transportation costs."

Philip scanned Robin's notes, snapping a nod of approval.

"If we can get some really competitive bidding going," Robin said, "we may not get stuck because of Quavely's shutdown."

"I'll need Adderly in on this," Philip said. "He's the man directly in charge of our construction."

"I have him standing by in the New Orleans office." Robin snapped the briefcase closed. "With luck, we can still be in production in the new plant in time for the next cane crop."

"Let's hope so." Philip reached and swung the attache case from the table. "I'll use the private phone in Huxley's study and start arranging some conference calls."

He turned to Diana, his eyes clinging for a warm second. "Thanks for the morning."

"It was a rare treat, Philip."

He gave her hand a parting squeeze. "See you later."

Robin coolly interposed herself, slipping a hand on Philip's arm. She insinuated him toward the door, taking a few steps with him. "Let me know when you're ready with the conference calls, darling."

Diana picked up the small stack of dishes. There were too few for the dishwasher, and she wouldn't leave them for Mrs. Lafarge, the apple-cheeked cook who was busy with afternoon marketing in the village.

Diana turned on the taps. Behind her, she heard the click of cup and saucer as Robin drifted to the coffee urn.

"Lucky you got in your ride." Robin's voice drifted from the table where she'd seated herself.

"Philip will be dreadfully busy for several days now with this aggravating Quavely thing."

Diana lifted dish-washing liquid from the shelf above the sink.

"But I suppose," Robin was going on in a silken little tone, "that Lucy's being bedridden will change your vacation plans. It promises a dreary summer, and I shouldn't blame you if you pack up as soon as you can gracefully do so."

Diana watched scalding water hiss over the dishes. The steam boiled up, a little like the aerosol inside of her. She had few pet hates, but one of them was the cruel barbarism of oh-so-civilized in-fighting. She could never think of the neat little cuts and thrusts, cover acid insolence with a condescending smile, say one thing when another was obviously meant.

"Thanks for the here's-hat-don't-hurry, Robin. But I rather like it here."

"Your prerogative." Robin shrugged.

Diana glanced over her shoulder, hands busy with the dishes. "I don't see an engagement ring on your finger. Shouldn't Philip have some small say-so in what he does with his spare time?"

"Philip is Acadian, and this is his place!" Spots of color had risen to Robin's velvety cheeks. "Philip's future is pretty well defined!"

And wouldn't you just wonder who wrote the script, Diana thought. She held back the state-

118

ment, seeing it as small and mean, and dried the few dishes, stacking them on the drain.

"Being a stranger, you haven't a notion of what's at stake," Robin was pressing on. "It's up to Philip to bring new vitality to Devereau House and all that it stands for. Add Devereau plantation, modernized and efficient, to Philip's present holdings and he would have the proper power base. He could move on, to become an economic giant in this state. And they are the men who rule, who choose the politicians and tell them what to do."

Diana gripped the sink, struck slightly numb by the power and determination of Robin's dream. No, more than a dream. A hunger. A fixation. An ambition that was frighteningly realistic.

A montage of Philip's future years blurred through Diana's mind. Could he withstand the careful, clever, ruthless manipulations of this captivatingly lovely woman? Or would she change him, so smoothly by degrees that he wouldn't recognize the substitution within himself of a personality that mirrored Robin's own? Would the virus of her ambition one day burn like a higher fever in him? Would he reach the point where he no longer would have to rationalize the gobbling of another parcel of land, a smaller refinery, a struggling shipping company? Where he would price-tag a public office with the remnants of a greedy politician's soul?

119

The tumble of thoughts brought a shiver to Diana's shoulders. Heaven help you, Philip . . .

She moved from the sink, steadied and controlled. Robin was watching her with calculating eyes and a stealthy little smile.

"You catch on quick, Diana."

"I can see how much you need Devereau plantation. But Huxley and Tony will have something to say about that, I imagine."

"Those two! Let them have their silly say!" Robin ground out. "A little water wears down a lot of stone. And we're hardly dealing with stone, but an uncertain pair who by accident of birth happen to bear the name of Devereau!"

Diana drew back from the ugliness working behind the smoothly beautiful face.

"Philip, by blood, is as much Devereau as Tony!" Robin was seething with the long-hidden sore point, her hand white-knuckled as she unconsciously tried to crush the nearest thing in her grasp, which happened to be the coffee cup. "By nature, Philip is more Devereau than the two of them put together! Left to Tony, what would become of all this, this house and all you can see out there? But Philip . . . Philip would use it!"

"If guided properly?" Diana suggested.

Robin flashed a look. Words almost came from her, but she didn't speak. She eased back in her chair, aware of how much she'd revealed in the heat of jealousy and anger. Her eyes strayed, returned. She was looking at Diana slyly. "If you have any ideas of repeating this conversation, I'd simply laugh it off and end up making you look like a meddling outsider."

"And I'm just about convinced you could do it," Diana agreed. She measured Robin from head to toe. "This does seem my day for talking with remarkable women."

"Really? Who was the other?"

"The woman in the red cottage where Philip and I stopped by. Domina."

Robin made a face. "Oh, her. With her money she could summer in Bar Harbor and winter on the Riviera. But I guess she enjoys the role of queen and seeress of the swamp people—and to stick around Huxley."

"She seemed courteous, nice—and talented."

"Darling," Robin said archly, "I think you are one of those people who looks at the world through rose-colored glasses. Domina is a freak-out, with too much nose for other people's business."

"Meaning that she influences Huxley against the merger of Nectar Sugar and Devereau interests?"

"Something like that." Robin shrugged her shoulders. "But little good it will do her. She should save her energies to play amateur psy-

121

choanalyst when Huxley comes down with a case of spiritual blahs. By the way, was he over there?"

"As a matter of fact, yes."

Robin affected a tolerant sigh. "While Tony cooled his heels waiting for his father. You see, that's an example of that pair. They were supposed to discuss business this morning. And where is Huxley? Off to chat with his lady friend."

Robin paused to let the implication sink in, of the future of Devereau plantation if left in inefficient hands.

"Well," she murmured shortly, "go right ahead and see Huxley as a sweet old man, Diana. You just don't know his history. Ask him sometime," Robin's eyes flickered with cunning, "about Prospera Clantell."

Prospera Clantell . . . the pixie face on canvas in the studio of the red cottage, Diana thought, the portrait painted a lifetime ago . . .

Prospera Clantell . . . Falling as it had from Robin's lips, the name seemed to evoke a shadow in Devereau House.

Chapter 8

The click of a door latch jarred the silence. Robin and Diana both turned. Tony was standing at the entry to the kitchen.

"Hi," he said, giving Robin a nod of careful courtesy. "What gives with Philip?"

"One of those endless business details." The change in Robin was little short of magical. She was at once nonchalant, quietly lovely, rather sweet. Her glance at Diana might have passed between casual friends. "Diana and I have had an interesting chat. But now I simply must run and see if Philip needs me for anything."

Tony held the door for Robin, and she passed him with a small, scrupulous smile of armed truce. He closed the door and slouched his fingers in the pockets of his jeans.

"Should have cut Philip out of your morning," he decided, "for all the good I did here."

"Cut him out?" Diana smiled. "Isn't there a third horse around?"

"There are a dozen horses around. But three riders is one too many."

"That's sweet of you, Tony."

"Yeah, that's me. Sweet old Tony."

Diana reached and took Tony's hand. "Walk me upstairs. I'm going to have another try at seeing Lucy."

"Speaking of seeing people, have you seen Cloty?"

"No. Why?"

"Abernathy asked me about her a few minutes ago, wanted Cloty to sit with Lucy a few minutes. I was looking for Cloty when I poked my head in here." He lifted his free hand and knuckled his lean jaw. "Come to think of it, I haven't seen Cloty since mid-morning. Not like the old gal to miss lunch."

"She's probably in the village pestering Constable Comage to come out and have another look around."

He stopped and turned her to face him, hands a rough touch on her shoulders. "What are you two hatching up?"

"Nothing, Tony. We're just not happy with the present answers."

His eyes flashed with dark life. His lanky tallness was towering. For an instant he was every inch the young master this house needed. "If you've turned up fresh evidence, don't you know it could be dangerous? You should have come to me!"

"I came to you first, Tony." Diana winced out of his grasp. "I told Cloty exactly what I told you, about Lucy's warning to me."

"And she acted on the strength of that?"

"Plus her own suspicions."

"What suspicions?" his words cracked. "Cloty hasn't told me . . ."

"Probably because you haven't asked her," Diana retorted. "And no doubt because she was certain you'd pass them off as the cranky workings of an old woman's mind." She paused for emphasis. "Cloty *feels* a desperate message in Lucy's eyes. She knows Lucy is trying to tell her something."

He drew a breath, enforcing male patience with the strange logic of womankind. "You call that evidence?"

Diana's eyes sparked. "You see? You note the masculine reaction?" she demanded, undaunted. "But regard us as you like, Tony. To me, Cloty's suspicions—as near and dear as she and Lucy have been for a lifetime—are as real as a chalk mark on a blackboard."

Her certitude gave him pause.

"Anyway," Diana added, "now there may be something else. I still think the accident with the pitchfork was suspiciously convenient."

His brow pinched a furrow. "What are you talking about?"

Diana related the incident at the barn in detail. As she did so, color seeped from Tony's cheeks and his face tightened in anxious lines.

"Diana!" He suddenly caught her to him and held her close. "Thank God you looked up in time!"

She heard the rasp of his breath. She hadn't meant to drive such a fright through him. She knew he was sick with the thought of what might have happened, chilled by the narrowness by which she'd escaped lying in the barnyard with the pitchfork handle protruding horribly from her.

His reaction brought the moment back to her, too clearly. In retrospective memory, the thought of those glinting, hurtling tines was even more nightmarish. Pressed against him, she accepted for a moment the shelter and warmth of his arms.

His hand stole up to touch and stroke her hair. "Maybe they don't thrive at Devereau House, the young and beautiful women," he whispered raggedly. "Maybe you've got to be a cypress stump like Abernathy, pruny and balding with a little gray topknot like Myree, or a jovial barrel like Mrs. Lafarge, the cook."

Diana stirred, looking up at the nearness of his face. "Old wive's fable, Tony."

"Maybe." He cupped her face with his hands, looked at her a long moment. "But if anything like

126

that happened to you, accidental or otherwise, I'd never forgive this house or anyone in it."

"Tony, you mustn't . . ."

His lips brushed the words away. His kiss was gentle, warm and tender. It was a quiet fire of joy, melting away the kitchen, dissolving for an instant the shadows of Devereau House.

He broke the kiss lingeringly. "Go away, Diana."

"No, Tony."

"It's the one unselfish thing I've said in quite awhile." His fingers lifted to brush a stray wisp of silken copper from her temple. "I don't know that I'll have the strength to say it again."

"Then don't, Tony. You know the decision isn't mine to make."

"All right," he muttered reluctant agreement. "The pitchfork could have happened like Philip said, the tool inching, stopping, pressing the hay under its own weight, inching another fraction, finally dropping. And . . ." he balked at the thought, "it could have been thrown from the concealment of the haymow. So you grow eyes in the back of your head, hear me?"

"Yes, Tony."

"Bolt your door at night. Scream at the top of your lungs at the slightest sound or shadow that doesn't belong. Don't worry about looking foolish."

"Yes, Tony," she laughed, his concerning,

strangely enough, breaking the thread of tension that had lurked in her since the moment in the barnyard.

From outside drifted the crackle of a foreign car engine. Tony cocked his head. The corners of his mouth tightened, and the moment of closeness was gone.

"Huxley," he surmised, "being returned to the menage by the lady guru."

Diana looked away from the subtle change in him, the stirring of restless and rebellious shadows through his face. He dropped his arms from her and crossed the kitchen to a small window overlooking the driveway.

"He's getting out of the car alone," Tony reported. "So I might as well talk to him. I've cooled my heels all day, waiting to do so."

He looked over his shoulder, his eyes smoky. Once more he was the slack-shouldered young Cajun, scorning the Establishment.

"Why don't we run off, get married, go live in hippie-ville? Chuck the whole thing? Let Philip have the headaches, the power, the glory? He— and Robin—will end up with it anyway."

"If I thought you meant that, Tony, I'd be ashamed for you."

"What makes you think I don't mean it? What's to stop me? Maybe you've cast my horoscope, being so sure of what I'll do."

"I'm not sure—but I think you'll stay and fight, Tony."

"For what?" His hand flung in a sweeping gesture. "A house ghosted with too many memories?"

"No, Tony. I think you'll find your own reasons for staying."

"Philip has offered some strong reasons for leaving," he said. "Like shares of stock. Like the whimsies of complete freedom on a juicy income without lifting a finger."

"Like the thought of what Robin will manage to do with the land—and the people on it," Diana rejoined. "Like the disappearance from this house of the Devereau name forever."

"Progress, Diana. All in the name of nice, civilized progress."

"Are you nicely civilized, Tony?" With a small wave of her hand, she left the kitchen, closing the door on whatever comeback he might have had.

She hurried up the broad curve of the main stairway and moved along the upper gallery. Her footsteps slowed as she approached the door of Lucy's room.

She listened with her ear against the panel, then pecked the door softly with her knuckles.

Nurse Abernathy responded, stalwart and solid in her crisp green uniform. Her slightly horse-like face reflected nothing, although she instantly divined the question in Diana's expectant eyes.

"Yes, Miss Latham, the doctor has been here.

Lucy is doing nicely." Breaking off, she admitted the smallest of smiles. "As a matter of fact, your visit seems to have helped Lucy, once the initial reaction passed."

"Then I may see her?"

"But no more of that excitement such as we had yesterday, understand me?"

"Chase me out at your pleasure," Diana smiled. "I'd be grateful for even a minute or two."

Abernathy nodded. "Let me cushion your arrival, then. I'll tell Lucy you are here."

The door clicked shut, and Diana waited impatiently. She could hear the muffled sound of Abernathy's voice as the nurse talked to Lucy.

Then Abernathy returned. "We won't stretch that minute or two very much," she warned. She stepped into the hall, clearing the way.

Diana braced herself, fastened a cheerful smile on her lips, and entered the sickroom. She heard the nurse close the door, leaving them alone.

The sight of Lucy's helpless, sheeted form was just as crushing as it had been yesterday; but prepared and conditioned by the previous visit, Diana managed to cross the room without faltering.

In the pert, gamin face, Lucy's expressive dark eyes sought Diana eagerly.

"Hi," Diana said, standing at bedside. Lucy's color appeared better. The ebony splash of her hair wasn't such a contrast to the paleness of her hollow cheeks.

Lucy winked a return greeting. Diana wouldn't let herself think of how heart-wrenchingly the eyelid movement substituted for the sound of that once vivacious voice.

Diana remained standing at the grotesquerie of the bed with its metal framing, ropes, pullies, and weights, none of which were in use at the moment.

She could feel Lucy's searching questions. She thought of keeping the opening gambit light, of sidling into questions of her own. But she wouldn't be fooling Lucy for a second, she knew.

"I've decided to ignore your warning," she said bluntly. "I'm staying at Devereau House."

And Lucy's eyes quickened with a reply: "I'm not surprised. You're a knuckle-head, you know."

"Sticks-and-stones," Diana smiled. "But your insults will never chase me."

And Lucy's eyes moistened: "I'm selfishly glad, Diana. But be careful, very careful."

"I'll test the air before I breathe it," Diana said. "But isn't there a chance you're wrong?"

And Lucy's eyes looked up, uncertain but challenging. She was saying: "A chance perhaps, but I don't think I'm wrong."

Diana felt a pulse triggering in her throat. "Then let's get to the nitty-gritty."

"Let's," Lucy's eyes agreed.

Diana was drawn a few inches closer to the head of the bed.

"We'll use the eyelid semaphore. One blink, yes. Two blinks, no."

Got it, Lucy blinked.

"We'll go back to the day of the accident. Had anything unusual or suspicious happened earlier here at the house?"

Two blinks.

"Just a normal day until you went to the chapel?"

Yes.

"Did you mention to anyone here where you were going?"

No.

"Did you leave the house alone?"

Yes.

Diana paused, resting a moment from the strain. Lucy looked up with the yearning wish that she could do better.

Diana fought back her sense of frustration. It was so difficult. The answers surely were all on the tip of Lucy's tongue. A tongue paralyzed and unable to speak.

"Let's reprise," Diana said. "You walked to the chapel and crossed to your favorite spot, below the St. Joan."

Yes.

"Did you go there every day?"

No.

"But frequently enough for someone to study your movements?"

Yes.

"Did you develop a habit pattern, going to the same spot in the chapel each time?"

Lucy drifted back in thought. Then signalled the answer: Yes.

"Therefore, someone who had watched and studied you could have predicted that the St. Joan statue, toppling at the right moment, would fall on you?"

Yes, Lucy blinked, and the fire in her eyes drove it home. Yes, yes, *yes!*

A smothering clutched Diana's throat. "Do you know who that person was?"

Painfully: No.

"Did anyone come into the chapel after you entered?"

No.

"But someone was watching from outside?"

Yes.

Diana paused and wiped her forehead with the back of her hand. She understood first-hand now what Cloty had meant about the message in Lucy's eyes. Lucy was trying so desperately to tell her how it had happened.

"Okay," Diana said with a fresh breath, "if the St. Joan didn't tip over of its own accord, it had to have the assistance of a human hand. Not much, with the mortar at the base rotted. Just a slight pressure, and the law of gravity would do the rest."

Yes.

"But you were alone in the chapel ruins. That places the human agency outside the walls."

Yes.

Diana paused, drawing away from the intensity of Lucy's eyes. There was no evidence the St. Joan had been booby-trapped. Even if the local constabulary had missed, the experts from New Orleans would have uncovered it.

Then how had the statue been given the necessary small impetus from outside the walls? Diana wondered.

She imagined herself in the shoes of the skulker. She built the scenes in her mind. She was seeing Lucy leave the house, knowing where Lucy was going and anticipating Lucy's precise movements when she got there.

Unseen by Lucy, the nameless, faceless skulker, making sure he wasn't observed, was slipping away from the house also. Slipping to the chapel with the cover of thickets and woods. Crawling close to the weedy walls. Lifting his eyes to watch Lucy inside the ruins through chinks between the stones where the mortar had rotted away.

And the simple answer came to Diana like a small explosion between her temples. The imaginary chapel scene vanished, and Diana was back, lips frozen apart, staring at Lucy.

"Anyone could have done it!" Diana gasped. "All he needed for a murder weapon was a long sliver of wood or a flat strip of scrap metal. He just slides it through a chink in the wall behind the St. Joan, touches the statue, and over it goes!" While you, Lucy, Diana's mind scorched with the thought, are squarely below the avalanche of stone . . .

Lucy's eyes closed and opened at last in a long-drawn yes.

"But why, Lucy? Do you know why anyone would do such a horrible thing?"

No.

I must end this, Diana thought. But the biggest question of all remained. It was a double-barrelled question, really. Part one: If Lucy had seen nothing, what evidence had caused her to conclude that someone had been outside the walls, urging the St. Joan to fall? Part two suggested itself in the event Lucy couldn't produce evidence, and Diana's mind shrank from this alternative question. Had Lucy, as Philip had suggested, built a paranoid delusion?

Diana would have preferred a nice, clean breakage of a bone to the present moment's kind of suffering. Philip's quietly objective and sensible words came hauntingly to her memory: Can a person suffer such a severe injury to the central nervous system and not have it affect her mind?

Diana went around the bed to the chair where Cloty read to Lucy. She saw her hand, surprisingly steady, touch the chair and shift its position.

She sat down, leaned forward, lifted Lucy's slightly usable right hand, and placed the waxen fingers on her upturned palm.

"What I must ask now, Lucy, can't be answered by a simple yes or no. We'll have to do it the hard way. Spell it out, letter by letter. You tap my palm as I go through the alphabet and reach the letter you have in mind, just as we did yesterday. Choose key words. Abbreviate. I can read back for a verification in the gaps."

Yes, Lucy blinked. Yes, get on with it, Diana!

Diana swallowed slowly, framing and rejecting questions in her mind, trying to cover the most ground in a single inquiry.

"It boils down to one point, Lucy. If anyone was close by the chapel, he would have heard the statue fall and, undoubtedly, your choked-off scream. He would have tried to help you—unless he wanted you dead. So the question is this. How can you be sure someone was out there?"

Lucy's eyes glowed with impatience, and Diana nodded a signal for the beginning.

"A . . ." Diana said. "B . . . C . . . D . . . E . . . F . . . G . . . H . . ."

Lucy's finger tapped.

"Second letter," Diana said. "A . . . B . . . C . . . D . . . E . . ."

Tap.

"H-e," Diana said. "He? Is that the word?"

Lucy blinked no.

"Okay, third letter. A . . ."

Quickly, Lucy's finger jerked.

"H-e-a . . ." Diana's eyes flicked up. "Head?"

No.

"Heard?"

Lucy blinked a bright, hard yes.

"You heard someone outside the ruined wall?"

Yes.

"Did he speak?"

No.

"Run away?"

Lucy's finger fluttered against Diana's palm, and Diana resumed the laborious alphabet. The soft, paced rhythm of her voice broke the acadian stillness. The sweeping second hand of the wall clock made its tireless rounds. And gradually the message formed. Bit by shadowy piece, the scene in the chapel ruins emerged, filling Diana with an anger she'd never thought herself capable of.

She sat back at last, not relaxing, a tautness binding through her limbs and posture.

"I'll play it back, Lucy, to make sure I haven't mistaken any of it." Diana drew in a breath. "You thought you were alone in the chapel. You heard a scratching from outside, behind St. Joan, thinking at first it was the rustling of a small animal of the woods. You glanced up, but too late. The statue was toppling. You screamed and tried to dive to one side. The stone struck you across the back. You had one long moment in which your senses fought to keep from going under. You heard a vicious laugh of satisfaction burst from someone's lips. That person was scrabbling over a break in the wall to make sure the trap had smashed its victim. Then before you actually saw the attacker, you couldn't hang on any longer, and lost consciousness."

Yes, Lucy blinked wanly, that's the way it happened.

And the rest of it is evilly obvious, Diana thought. Fearing the chance that Lucy's brief scream might have been heard, the attacker had taken time for one quick look before vanishing. It was enough to glut a pair of avid eyes with an overwhelming sense of success. The small, still form, crushed beneath a ton of stone, gave every appearance of death.

The thought came to Diana that no one could have survived. But Lucy had. Lucy with her child-like faith, her love of humanity, her quest for strengthening by a power above and beyond herself . . .

Diana pushed to her feet. "I'll let you rest now. And you mustn't worry. We'll see it through, I know we will. And the visits then will be a lot different."

Luck winked an A-OK, and Diana managed to match it with a nervy smile.

Outside the room, Diana saw Cloty coming along the gallery. They hurried to meet.

138

The spare old governess was wearing her sternly irascible look. "I sneaked to the village. But our fine-feathered Constable Comage is off in the parish swamps chasing a pair of illegal moon-shiners."

Diana glanced back and forth, making sure they were alone. She reported her session with Lucy.

Cloty's eyes snapped. "Good! That eases my disappointment at missing the constable. Now I'll have something solid to tell him! I'll ease back into the village first thing tomorrow morning."

Cloty fingered the spectacles that dangled from their neck chain. "Now that we've something tangible to bestir Comage, it might be safer if you let on like you didn't get anything more from Lucy." She wagged a finger. "Now mind you, child, I'm not suggesting bald-faced lies. Just gloss the truth over a little."

Diana nodded, not suppressing her smile. "I was thinking of the same thing."

Cloty lifted her glasses, peered. "I think we make a team, you and I. The fox is cunning. But I think we shall make some smoke for the den!"

Diana heard a door open nearby and turned her head. Abernathy had come from the bedroom suite set aside for nurse's quarters.

"Have a good visit?"

"It was nice, just seeing her," Diana said. "We

had a chat, in our fingertap code, but she couldn't tell me as much as I had hoped."

Cloty gave Diana a hidden elbow nudge that said nicely glossed.

Abernathy had shifted her hazel eyes to the old governess. "Since you haven't been in today, I suppose you'd like to keep the train of visitors moving."

"I would, indeed. I'll read the child to sleep." Cloty marched off in the direction of Lucy's room, Abernathy plodding elephantine in her wake.

The remainder of the day slipped by uneventfully. After dinner, Diana made a fourth at bridge with Huxley, Philip, and Robin.

Robin was sleekly golden and charmingly gracious. Her manner carried no hint that she and Diana had crossed verbal swords. Instead, she set about lacerating Diana at the bridge table. She was a marvelous player, confident, computerized in her judgments of odds and card locations.

Diana didn't so much mind coming off the short end of the scoring at the evening's end. She'd been outplayed and fairly beaten. But it did rankle, as Robin intended, to have Robin apologizing to the men for her: "A break in trump and she might have made the diamond bid . . . Huxley, you really shouldn't have raised her to slam . . . Diana's club lead seemed perfect against my four-spades bid. Lucky for me it was to my void suit . . ."

Huxley mixed nightcaps and as the evening was breaking up, Philip walked Diana upstairs. They stood in the dimness of the gallery.

"She's quite a woman," Diana remarked.

"Robin? Yes," Philip nodded, "she's got a lot going for her. Growing up together, the combination has always seemed natural, families being friends, belonging to the same clubs and all that."

He nestled Diana's chin in his hand and lifted her face slightly. "But now," he grinned, "I'm not sure Robin's my druthers."

"Philip, you mustn't . . ."

"Why not say what I feel? Everything was taken for granted for Robin and me, until you came like a fresh breeze to Devereau House."

His eyes caressed her face. "Let's give ourselves a chance to know each other better. That's all I'm asking."

"I think I'd like that, Philip."

He kissed her with quiet respect. "Pleasant dreams."

"Good night, Philip."

She watched him stride down the stairway before she went into her rooms. She leaned against the door, searching into herself. She thought about Tony and Philip and the differences in them. Tony with his uncertainties and mercurial moods and Philip with his feet solidly on the ground. She wondered wryly why each in his own way had to be so attractive.

141

Later, when Diana was settled between crisp sheets, it was thoughts of Lucy that came stealing out of the silent darkness.

Did Lucy imagine demonic laughter in the maculating instant of St. Joan's crash?

No, Diana thought, I can't buy it like that. Sure, Lucy was looking for some answers about life—and haven't we all. But the need to think things out in a quiet place doesn't mean she was so freaked out that she imagined ghostly cacklings. Lucy's as sane, Diana decided, as . . . well, Philip.

Lucy's story was for real. Someone else had been out there at the chapel, deliberately nudging the statue from outside the ruined wall.

And up jumped the horns of an ugly paradox.

Tony had said it.

No one had a reason for destroying Lucy. But someone had tried.

Diana tossed, restive. Did Lucy's present helpless condition satisfy the unknown motive? Or did she remain an obstacle to an enigmatic purpose? Was another person in Devereau House right now thinking of Lucy, figuring a safe way of getting to her and finishing the job?

Diana slept at last, and awakened with a touch of surprise that birds should be singing so happily in the sunlight outside her window.

Chapter 9

On her way to breakfast, Diana detoured by Lucy's room. The nurse gave Diana a scanty minute at Lucy's bedside before bustling her out with reminders of linens to change and intravenous feedings to prepare.

A vivid auburn-haired image in a sensibly cool white cotton dress and sandals, Diana nodded to herself as she descended the broad and gentle curvature of the main stairway. At least Lucy looked none the worse for the ordeal of yesterday's interrogation.

Huxley Devereau spoke Diana's name from the upper gallery, and she paused halfway down to wait for him.

They continued on to breakfast side by side, the limping old man escorting her with a natural, but aged, savoir faire.

Conversation was a casual pleasantry during

first coffee and grapefruit touched with sherry and powdered sugar. Hearty and jovial, uniformed so crisply white it seemed she must crackle with each movement, Mrs. Lafarge brought in servings of eggs benedict.

"Domina was quite taken with you, Diana," Huxley remarked. He had seated her at the corner of the fine old dining room table, next to his place at the head of the table. "She is serious in her wish to paint you. Would you mind sitting for her? Not as a choresome duty. Just when you want to change the pace as the summer passes."

"I'd like to. But can I risk it?" Diana smiled.

"Risk it?"

"Whatever she might reveal in my face. She has a penetrating brush."

"She does indeed." Huxley reached and patted her hand. "But in you Domina would see what Lucy first saw, the inner beauty we've all now had a chance to see."

"Thank you for that, Huxley. It's one of the nicest compliments I've ever had."

"Not a compliment," he growled. "Statement of fact. You are real, Diana. A vain or pretentious woman would have responded with an inane remark. Such as, 'You'll have me blushing, Huxley,' or 'Flattery will get you anyplace, Huxley.' "

"My own reply wouldn't have won prizes for originality."

"But it was sincere. It paid me the honor of candidly accepting what I had to say." Huxley forked a bit of English muffin from his plate. "Shall I tell Domina to clean her brushes?"

Diana nodded acceptance. "It would be fun."

"Good."

"I haven't the trained eye of a critic, but I think her work is terrific," Diana said. "One that kind of haunts me . . . a very old one . . . the face of a girl. Prospera Clantell."

Voicing the remark in all innocence, Diana was stunned by the old man's reaction. He choked. The line-webbed parchment of his face went absolutely white. He clutched his silver in blue-veined talons that trembled. But instead of glazing with faintness, his eyes came up flashing violet fire. His mouth opened on a near roar, "What do you know about Prospera Clantell?"

"Why, nothing, Huxley."

He stared at the bewilderment in her face, and began getting hold of himself with a quivering effort. "I didn't know the old painting was still in her studio," his voice dropped to a grumbling lameness. "Just a long-ago memory, Diana . . . nothing to concern you."

He looked at his hands bonded about knife and fork and forced his fingers to relax. "There are few taboos in Devereau House, but that name— Prospera Clantell . . . I'd appreciate it if you wouldn't mention it again."

"Huxley, truly I didn't know I was . . ."

"You did nothing," he said, voice back on a normal track. "So please forget it."

"Of course, Huxley."

His gaze crept back to her. A coaxing smile slipped across his lips. "Forgive a cranky old galoot for shouting at you?"

"How can I resist? Full clemency," she laughed, but didn't feel it inside.

He buried the subject with an abrupt switch to talk of horses and the pinto Diana had ridden yesterday.

After breakfast, Diana returned upstairs. She was thankful none of the others had joined her and Huxley, dragging out breakfast. She had risen early because two bits of business had lurked in her mind, awakening her this morning.

The first chore was simple. She tapped softly on Cloty's door. Receiving no response, she cracked the door and peeked in. Across the pleasant clutter of the old lady's room Cloty's bed was rumpled, and empty. Diana emitted a small breath of satisfaction. Cloty was already up and about—on her way to light a fire under Constable Comage.

Diana closed the door and hurried along the gallery. The second task, she reflected, was more involved and would take longer.

She left the house by the narrow rear stairs she and Tony had first used. The summer sun was well up, but a dewy freshness lingered in the air. Off in

146

the marshes the last tendrils of mists were dissolving.

Diana moved away from the house as if taking a random morning stroll. Idling about the landscape, her gaze included the white walls and towering twin chimneys. No one else was visible on the grounds, and she didn't think she'd been observed from the house.

When the shadows of the pines cut her off from the house, her pace quickened on the dim path. Thickets, brambles, tree trunks, the blaze of wild flowers fled past. The dark, forbidding hulk of the Devereau family mausoleum reared in the edge of her vision and then was behind her.

She was a little breathless when she drew up before the ruins of the chapel. A swampy silence oozed about her. Through the broken jumble of the front portal she could see shafts of sunlight probing the dankness of decayed pews and altar.

She jerked back, startled, as a lizard-like creature skittered almost underfoot, a green and orange flash burrowing beneath the rot of a collapsed, snail-ridden timber.

"Ninny!" she scolded herself with a shallow breath.

She moved to the left, picking her way through wild vines that tangled underfoot and concealed shards of broken tiles from a once-existent roof.

Slowly, she worked her way alongside the chapel wall, pausing twice to look back and judge distances. The third time she stopped, she was, by simple reckoning, directly outside the niche where the statue had stood.

She studied the base of the wall and saw a crushed fern or broken weed here and there. Telltale traces of Ozar Fant, she surmised, made when the gargoyle-faced old man had spied on her and Tony.

A dry twig cracked underfoot as she pressed against the wall. With a slight stretch, she levelled her eyes at a crack between the rough stones. It was several inches long and fully a quarter of an inch wide, where mortar had turned to powder and ridden away on the winds of decades.

A drawn coldness gathered in her nape. Through the crack she could see the altar, and the broken mass of St. Joan. By inching her head and bringing one eye against the crack she could even glimpse the forward edge of the niche where the statue had stood.

She was held for a moment; then she backed away with stiff, careful steps. No need, she thought, to test the theory any further. The crack was more than ample for anyone to have nudged the statue with a thrust from outside. Anyone could have planned it in advance, knowing Lucy would return. Anyone could have stolen into the ruins ahead of time and made sure the statue was on a needlepoint balance. Anyone who was a fiend . . .

Now that she was finished, Diana turned quickly, feeling she never wanted to see the place again. But she determined to do so. She would see it when she and Cloty brought Constable Comage here.

Her discovery at the chapel and the images it evoked left her with a feeling of tiredness. She wended slowly from the chapel, along the wooded path. Near the hulking mass of the Devereau burial crypt, she paused, hesitant, wondering if she had actually heard a rustling in the vicinity of the mausoleum.

She scanned the weathered tomb, the underbrush encroaching upon it. The day was as pleasant as a poem, friendly clouds puffing a blue sky, sunlight beaming through the trees, birds singing.

Then as she was about to go, Diana noticed a glitter of light a few feet away. It came from just off the path, closer to the mausoleum, a hard needle of reflected sunlight.

She stepped from the path, slippery pine needles whispering a protest. Then she identified the beacon . . . a pair of spectacles, one lens broken, the other intact and gathering a filter of sunlight into a diamond hardness.

Diana gasped and dropped to one knee. Her hand thrust out and shook slightly as she lifted the spectacles. The fine links of the neck chain shimmered in the sunlight. No mistaking the glasses . . . they belonged to Cloty.

Diana's hand folded on the spectacles tightly. She straightened up, staring at the mausoleum. That tiny sound . . . Had it come from inside the vault? Was Cloty in there?

Diana fought a shudder, forcing herself to move. The mausoleum seemed to swim toward her. She stood poised a few feet from the rusty, iron-barred entry. The two sections of the lattice-like gateway were unbolted, standing open by three or four inches.

"Cloty?" It was a husk that Diana hardly heard herself. She edged another yard forward, straining to see inside the crypt. The sun was in the wrong position, and the depths were black. A chill seeped out, driving a shiver through Diana.

She stood there dry-mouthed and unable to swallow.

"Cloty?"

The thought of entering that dark, closed space filled her with a sickening vertigo. It was too much like a stifling closet with a bolted door closing in about a terror-stricken child. And the memory of her own voice, wailing a plea to her foster-father, came reeling out of the deep past: "No, no, daddy . . . please let me out . . . there are *things* in here, daddy . . . I'll be a good girl, only let me out . . ."

Diana took a step back, looking about frantically. Nothing. No one.

Where is Cloty, if not in there?

No, no . . . I'll run to the house . . . But it's quite a way, there and back. And what if you don't find someone right away? Cloty may be dying . . . Want to remember, for the rest of your life, that you might have saved her?

I can't . . .

You must. You will. You're not a child. It's not a silly closet.

The two vehement parts of her mind burst back together. With a shock, she saw her hands tugging at the iron doors, pulling them further apart.

Her brain seemed to float. She was a little way inside.

"Cloty?" The ragged word echoed faintly. To her right and left, Diana could make out stone slabs that enclosed Devereaus in eternal rest. But beyond the entry, the haze from outside dimmed to nothingness.

She ventured another few steps. If she only had a light, a commonplace packet of matches . . .

And then she was spinning about, a scream twisting her lips as the iron doors clanged shut. She was all stone and ice for a moment. It was as if she had stepped from herself. She knew someone was out there. In the small geometric openings in the latticed iron gate she glimpsed bits of a shadowy figure in frantic motion. But it didn't connect up. Her paralyzed mind refused to give it meaning.

The instant was shorter than a heartbeat, but it

151

seemed an age before she broke the trance, realizing that the fragmentary figure had bolted the gate and fled.

She threw herself against the barrier, and the rusty iron smashed her backward.

Her senses were spinning, a blackness sweeping over her eyes. Dimly, she knew she was kicking and beating against the unyielding metal. She heard her voice shrieking and breaking against the walls of the tomb: "Let me out . . . Please . . . I'll be a good girl . . . Only let me out, daddy . . ."

She sagged against the gate, fingers curled in the rough ironwork for support, knees collapsing. Sheathed in clamminess, she clung there fighting for breath.

Daddy? she thought. What am I saying? What am I doing to myself?

A tremor of anger sparked through her. This is crazy, she thought, blind panic. A foster-father and a locked closet were a long time ago. This was now.

The little girl, Diana, she told herself, she's just a memory. The closet was just a closet.

And this place . . .

A tinge of strength touched her knees. Just a place, Diana. Morbid place, dreary place. Nothing more, nothing less. What's in here to hurt you?

She giggled a laugh. The people certainly can't . . .

A strange new feeling began to warm her. She loosened her fingers, one by one like bands breaking. Gradually, she stood, steady on her feet, a clarity taking hold of her mind.

She didn't move for a quiet moment, trying to make sense of her emotions. She was locked in, but felt oddly free. She wanted out, but with a desperation normal to the circumstance. The gibbering terror of a closed space was gone.

I faced you, little girl in the closet, she thought, and you need never be afraid again . . .

She drew a calm breath. She could mull over the shock treatment and the intracacies of the human psyche at a more appropriate time. Right now, the problem was to get out. The attacker might return—with a weapon.

She thrust her fingers through an aperture and tried to reach the outside bolt. She could feel its tip. Biting her lip, she forced her hand a fraction further. There it stuck, the rough metal crushing her knuckles.

She groped and strained her fingers like writhing and blind caterpillars. Her nails grated on the end of the bolt. It remained fast.

She paused, her mind bearing down on the situation. If I had something, she thought, to extend my reach . . .

Cloty's spectacles! The thought chilled pleasantly. She'd ventured in with the broken glasses in her hand. They must still be in here, dropped or hurled away in the moment of blind panic. If she could engage a piece of the frame or the neck chain, she might be able to slip the bolt.

"M'am, you need some fetchin' help, 'pears like."

Diana abrased her knuckles in startled reaction to the nasal, Cajun twang from outside. She pressed her face against the grating, and saw the lanky, overalled figure of Ozar Fant standing a dozen feet away in a splash of sunlight.

For an instant, his misshapen face was almost beautiful. Then Diana was cautioned by the question of what he was doing so close to the mausoleum.

She stood nursing her skinned knuckles with her other palm. "Mr. Fant," she requested calmly, "please slip the bolt."

"Well, now, I reckon I might. Least-ways it's worth a thought. You're Miss Latham in there, ain't you?"

"Yes. And what's to think over, Mr. Fant? All I want you to do is flip the bolt."

"Please, m'am, not so fast." He was wearing an old felt hat, greasily soiled and tattered in the crease of the crown. He thumbed the floppy brim back. "A-fore you paddle the bayou, Miss Latham, you make sure the boat ain't leaking."

"What kind of talk is this? If it's money you want, I'd be glad to pay you."

154

He lifted a calloused palm. "Don't prick my pride, lady," he warned. "I ain't a beggar."

He shuffled a few steps closer, his weirdly askew eyes peering. "I've asked about you, Miss Latham. Fine young lady visitor to Devereau House is well talked over in the village. I know you and Miss Lucy was partners in that Peace Corps work. I can reckon how you feel about such a friend. But, m'am, you ought to realize you can't do nothing for her." He rubbed his lantern-jawed face. "Just bring on yourself a passel of trouble, that's all."

Diana fought away the thought of him walking off and leaving her locked in. She sensed he was driving at a bargain of some kind.

"Mr. Fant," she tried to keep the faltering note from her voice, "if you locked me in here to lay down terms of some kind . . ."

His mouth fell agape. "M'am, I swear I didn't throw the doors on you! I heard you holler. Just the once. Like the dead in there was coming to life. I come on the trot to see."

"Then what is it you want?"

He slipped off the hat and fingered sweat from the inner band. He mused on her with one eye while the other seemed to drift in space.

"Want?" he said finally. "Funny you should ask. Nobody much ever asked what Ozar Fant wants. But I don't mind revealing myself, m'am, gospel truth."

His voice dropped to a painful level of sincerity. "I just want things to be nice for folks. You know? I don't mean frilly clothes or fancy cars. I don't want nobody hurt. I want no more suffering, m'am."

Diana was held to silence. Was he really an old devil? Or a saintly soul in repulsive disguise?

"You see, m'am," he warned, "they's dark things in Devereau House best left at rest. But I hanker a feeling you ain't a restful person. For Miss Lucy's sake, you're going to have to stick your pretty nose in, and you might get it chopped off."

"I don't understand, Mr. Fant."

"Lady," he said crossly, "you understand too much a-ready. You should never have come here. If you got a grain of sense, you'll go right back where you came from!"

"I can't very well go anywhere right now, Mr. Fant."

"Then see that you do!" he snarled. He stabbed a hand, and the latch bar grated in its slit. He gave a tug, and the sections of the gate swung out with a rusty groan of protest.

Breath caught, Diana watched the space widen. She slipped through and turned to speak to Fant. But he looked at her with flashing eyes and raised a knotted fist at the end of a big-knuckled wrist.

"Git!" he thundered. "Git while there is time. Git far—and never come back!"

Diana fell back, almost losing her footing. Then she was scrambling into a run. She ignored clutching brambles and thickets, gulping hot spears of breath into her lungs, running toward the white patches of Devereau House distantly seen through the trees.

Chapter 10

Disheveled and breathless, Diana saw no one about as the shadows of the house fell across her. The patio was deserted, the swimming pool like a huge pane of glass, the playroom silent beyond closed glass doors.

Diana yanked the rear door of the kitchen and almost fell inside. Old Myree was at the sink scouring utensils. Her moth-eaten gray topknot jerked up and a pot clattered from her hands, Diana's explosive appearance visibly startling her.

Diana slumped against the door jamb. Drying her hands on her apron, Myree came across the kitchen in a wary, timid shuffle. She was wide-eyed. "What happened? You fall down a gully or something?"

Diana pushed a tangle of hair from her cheek with the back of her hand. She realized that her headlong flight had left her looking like a ragdoll a pair of kittens had fought over. Little wonder her wild arrival had spooked the edgy old menial.

"I'm all right, Myree," she assured, "as soon as I get my breath back."

Myree queried an unconvinced look. "You better sit down and have a glass of water."

It sounded like a good idea. Diana moved limply to the table and eased onto a chair. Slipping worried glances over her shoulder, Myree lifted a pitcher from the refrigerator and poured a glass of water.

"There now. Ice cold. You'll feel better."

"Thank you," Diana said, taking the glass from Myree's out-thrust hand. "Please see if you can find Philip or Tony for me."

Myree bobbed a nod and scurried toward the inner doorway. She had almost slipped through when Diana's voice caught her. "Myree . . ."

The servant drew up, looked back. "Yes, m'am?"

"Did you happen to see anyone, besides myself, leave the house a little earlier and head toward the woods?"

"Didn't pay no particular notice. Been busy."

"It would help, Myree."

The scrawny old woman fingered her topknot. "Didn't see nobody out back, except Mr. Tony."

"Tony?" Diana set down her half-empty glass. "Where?"

"Out yonder." Myree made a vague motion that

included a lot of acreage. "Just taking a walk. He often does when the restlessness is on him."

Tony? Diana frowned to herself. "Did he go off in the direction of the old chapel?"

"Can't say that he did. Can't say that he didn't. Is that all, m'am?"

Diana's head moved in an uncertain nod. Vaguely, she heard Myree go out. She sat staring without real focus on the red-brick kitchen floor. Tony in the woods? Tony slamming the iron portals of the mausoleum?

Diana's teeth clicked together. No! The very thought was preposterous. If the ridiculous chain of thought was followed, it meant that Tony must have been the stalker outside the ruined chapel on Lucy's fateful day. It suggested that Tony had tipped the statue onto his own sister.

Diana shivered, sick with herself for even toying with such thoughts. Of all the people in this house, it was Tony who loved Lucy the most.

Diana's head snapped up as she heard footsteps hurrying toward the kitchen. She stood, seeing Philip's wide-shouldered figure framed in the doorway.

He hurried on toward her, his eyes taking in details. "Are you all right, Diana? Myree burst in with a tale of your looking like you'd chased brer rabbit through a briar patch."

"I'm fine," Diana said quickly. Before she could

160

say more, Tony and Robin came crowding up worriedly beside Philip.

She looked at their faces, forcing a reassuring smile. "I had a fright, that's all. I was . . . taking a stroll. I found Cloty's glasses, broken, near the mausoleum I heard a sound that I thought came from in there. I ventured in—and someone slammed the gate on me."

Philip paled. "Diana!"

Tony gritted his teeth. "What a rotten trick!"

Even Robin was moved to a sympathetic cluck. "How awful! How did you manage to get out?"

"The old bayou squatter, Ozar Fant, came along and unbolted the doors."

Philip wedged a shoulder between Diana and Tony, and led her to chair.

"Let's put this thing together rationally," he said, his voice steady as an anchor, "and see . . ."

"You rationalize!" Tony burst out. "I'm going to have a look for Cloty!" He spun on his heel and started out.

"Just a minute!" Philip's voice stopped Tony. "We'll all be having a look for Cloty."

Philip and Tony faced each other across the space of the kitchen. The tension between them hinted at an old and long-drawn struggle. Philip's eyes demanded that Tony recognize and observe the chain of command.

A muscle quivered in Tony's jaw. "Order your own people, Philip," he said quietly. "I don't happen to be one of them!"

The squared-off moment held; then Philip parried it aside with a small, tolerant smile. He took Diana's hand. "Come along," he said. "You can fill us in with the details on the way."

Diana told them almost all of it while the small party hurried from the house. She omitted her observations at the chapel, deciding that her solution of a would-be murderer's method should await the ears of Comage, the law.

The verdant surroundings were serene when the group arrived at the crypt.

They stood bunched close to Diana. "I found Cloty's spectacles over there," she said, pointing. "I had them in my hand when I came over and walked in. I dropped them somewhere in there. When Fant released me, I was so glad to get away I didn't think of anything else until I was back at the house."

"Then the glasses are still inside," Robin remarked.

Tony was swinging wide the two sections of the gate. He and Philip entered, scanning the dusty, stone-slab floor.

They paused, faced by the gloom of the deeper interior. "You must have given them a wild toss, Diana," Philip mused. He slipped a butane lighter from his pocket, sparked it, and turned the flame to full high.

Diana edged to the entrance, Robin lingering behind her. Diana felt the heavy air of the tomb, watching Philip's feeble torch recede. The flickering light wavered the shadows of the two men, silhouettes in weird motion as they searched.

Diana's nails crunched gradually in her palms as she watched the feeble pool of light creep over the empty floor. Philip was methodical, careful, patient, holding the light low to the floor, missing not a crack.

Then he and Tony were brought up by the solid rock walling the mausoleum in the rear. They straightened, their faces pale, floating ovals in the instant before Philip snapped off the lighter.

They resolved out of the gloom, faces adding the reality of arms, legs, bodies. Tony kneaded a kink in the small of his back from his bent-over search. Philip's evenly hewn face gathered a frown.

"Cloty's spectacles are just not in there, Diana," Philip said.

"Are you sure you carried them in?" Robin asked. Her tone was saccharine sweet, and Diana gritted her teeth. If Philip or Tony had asked the same question, Diana might have said that she wasn't quite so sure now. Details of the dreadful experience wanted to blur, to dart out of memory.

Robin sensed her swirl of uncertainty. "Perhaps you're not positive you entered the crypt at all, Diana."

Diana turned on her. "That one had some earmarks, Miss Toutain."

Robin moved her trim shoulders in a small shrug. "Well, after all, if I'd found Cloty's glasses and heard a suspicious sound, I'd have thought twice before going in that place."

"I thought more than twice," Diana said. "I wouldn't have dreamed of walking in the crypt if I hadn't thought Cloty might be in there seriously hurt."

"You're a very brave girl," Robin murmured.

The creamy face seemed to distort in Diana's vision. She's slipping out her weapons, Diana thought, and it's not my style of fighting.

Fatigued and vexed, she wondered if Devereau House and all that it implied wasn't too much for her. "You're right, Robin. I was brave! I found the glasses—and I went into the crypt!"

"Diana . . ." Tony said.

She shook off his touch. "Believe me or don't—it's up to you."

"Of course we believe you," Philip said. "You've had a trying experience. A little aftermath of hysteria is normal."

Was that, in truth, the way he regarded her? Diana drew a limp breath, feeling isolated, ringed-in. "Hysteria, Philip?"

He grasped her hand, grinning crookedly. "Big mouth, big foot in it. I didn't mean it quite that way, Diana."

She saw the concern in his eyes. But it was anxiety for her, more than for things she reported and couldn't substantiate, such as a falling pitchfork that left no marks in the earth and broken spectacles that didn't exist.

"Why," she asked quietly, "would I report something that didn't happen here? What reason could I have?"

"Good questions," Robin said before Philip or Tony could speak. "And a better one might be why you came to Devereau House in the first place."

Robin's words left a silence hanging in the tree-shadowed clearing.

Diana drew her hand from Philip's. So Devereau House had questions about her, just as she had for it.

Her lips were stiff. "Is that worth an answer, Robin?"

"Why not?" Robin's golden head reflected a fire of sunlight. "You seem to be doing your best to tip over applecarts. Things were peaceful at Devereau House, until you came. We've all felt the change. Quite handily, you've set us all against each other with your talk of secrets exchanged in Lucy's room, your claim that her accident wasn't an accident at all, but attempted murder."

165

"Pete's sake, Robin," Tony spoke up at last. "You don't know what you're saying."

"I know quite well," Robin said with an air of pointed patience. "You must have asked yourself the same questions. Hasn't the conveniently timed arrival of a stranger seemed the least bit odd? How do you—we—know she's Diana Latham in the first place? Can Lucy walk out of her room and tell us?"

It was even worse when Philip put a fond hand on Diana's shoulder and said reassuringly, "Come now, Robin, I'm sure Diana can prove she is Diana."

The corner of Diana's mouth tugged bitterly. "Has it reached the point where proof is needed?"

"It might help," Robin said, "in view of all that's happened."

Break it off, Diana thought, and leave her wicked little traps for someone else. But how did everyone else feel? Were they, from cook to master, beginning to view her with puzzlement?

"If I'm not Diana Latham, who am I?"

"Perhaps someone who knew Diana Latham," Robin said, "someone quick to read opportunity into Diana Latham's connection with the rich, generous, and trusting Devereaus."

Diana stared, and Robin met her gaze unyieldingly. Diana felt twin fires in her cheeks. "This is preposterous! An imposter wouldn't dare walk in and face Lucy."

166

"That's the very thing an imposter would do," Robin suggested. "Who knows what you said to Lucy? You could have told her that you were a dear friend of Diana Latham's, arriving in her stead. It would have been no trick to gain the confidence of a helpless, lonely, and mute Lucy."

"But I didn't know about Lucy's condition, until the moment I arrived."

"Really?" Robin arched a brow. "Lucy's accident, and the investigation, got a lot of newspaper coverage."

Diana was stunned to lame silence by the picture Robin was painting. Of an imposter. Of a cunning scheme, not yet revealed but already in operation.

It was nonsensical—except that in the brooding uncertainties rampant in Devereau House it was more believable than some of the things Diana had herself witnessed.

Robin's face hovered, cool and remote. She's like some old spidery politician mis-using his committee powers to destroy a hapless victim with innuendo, Diana thought. Every bit as wily. Equally merciless. How can the surface woman be so lovely?

Diana shook her head. "You'll have to believe that the Kansas papers didn't carry a line about Lucy's accident. And," she tried to lighten it, "I don't happen to subscribe to the New Orleans dailies."

Philip slipped his arm about her shoulders. "We're all a little upset. I think we'll feel better when Cloty comes stomping in to report the loss of her glasses."

"Robin should be feeling great already," Tony added.

Diana wished their solicitude had been a little more spontaneous. As she turned to go, she glimpsed Robin's face. It glinted with satisfaction. The fact that Tony and Philip hovered beside Diana during the walk to the house didn't bother Robin at all. She's planted her weeds, Diana thought. Now all she has to do is prune them and watch them grow.

Diana said nothing more until the group had entered the playroom. She crossed to the wall phone and was lifting it from the hook when Philip hurried over beside her. Tony went drifting from the room, and Robin dawdled toward the bar keeping an eye on Philip and Diana.

"Comage?" Philip asked, hovering close by her side.

Diana nodded.

Philip glanced at the phone as if he would make the call to the constable himself. "Don't you think we should first check the house? It would be embarrassing if we got Comage out here and Cloty came snorting into the room."

"I think Tony is already off in the role of bloodhound," Robin remarked from the bar. With brazen aplomb, she tossed a silken smile at Diana. "Care for a tall, frosty drink, darling?"

"No thanks." Diana let the phone slip back in place. Philip moved to the bar, accepting from Robin a chilled glass.

Diana lingered near the phone, and when Tony returned presently, she knew from a look at his face that Cloty wasn't in the house.

"She hasn't shown at Lucy's room all day, either," Tony said.

Diana placed the call, and a resonant Cajun baritone responded: "Constable's office. Comage speaking."

"This is Diana Latham. I'm . . ."

"I know, Miss. The guest at Devereau House. Lucy's friend. I've intended to drop by and pay my respects, but it's an ornery parish that keeps me busy. What can I do for you?"

"Have you seen Miss Clotilde Mathis today?"

"Haven't seen Cloty in quite awhile, Miss. But I expect to. I understand she called this office yesterday."

Diana gripped the phone tightly. "Can I see you right away, Constable Comage?"

He seemed to sense urgency in the very quietude of her voice. "Are you at Devereau House?"

"Yes."

"I'll be right out."

"Thank you, very much."

The line went dead, and Diana hung up slowly.

169

Comage had sounded decisive and capable. It helped, when one felt beleagured.

Talk was scanty while the group waited for Comage. Poor Tony and Philip, Diana thought, trapped in the gap of strained civility between Robin and me.

Presently, Comage was shown into the playroom by Lafarge, the pleasant middle-aged manservant.

Tony was brooding at the tall glass doors looking out on the pool, fingers thrust in the hip pockets of his jeans. Robin, at ease in a deep chair, glanced up from the magazine she was idling through. Out of the room briefly, Philip entered almost on the constable's heels.

"Hello, Pierre," Philip said.

The constable half turned. "How are you, Philip?" Comage nodded at Tony and Robin in turn. Then his eyes rested on Diana as she crossed the room.

He was a robust man, tall and meaty, in a simple uniform of gray twill trousers, a wide black belt supporting girth, gun, and handcuffs, and a short-sleeved gray shirt with a constable's patch on the shoulder. He was carrying a flat-brimmed stetson in huge, freckle-splotched hands. His face was large and florid, hinting at dewlaps. He had a ready smile, and Diana suspected his laugh would boom on occasion. His eyes were small and sharp, buried in deep crow's feet. His bald head showed flecks of sun-burned peel, and he had two quaint little tufts of wiry red hair growing out of his ears.

Comage's handshake, as Philip introduced Diana, had a burry roughness, pleasantly suggesting a tolerant strength.

"Now, Miss Latham, what's this about Cloty?"

He listened gravely while Diana touched the high points. A flick of those puckered eyes silenced interruptions, and when Diana had made her statement, he took her arm and guided her toward the glass doors.

"You folks make yourselves to home while Miss Latham and I have a second look." With that, he ushered Diana from the house.

His drawling baritone rambled on commonplaces as he and Diana walked the distance to the mausoleum. He mentioned the weather, asking how it compared with the mountains of Peru. He had relatives in Kansas and knew Bankhead's Crossing. He talked about the long drive down in a compact car such as Diana owned. He remarked on Philip's horsemanship and the state of Huxley's health.

His statements were cleverly leading, incomplete without responses. By the time they reached the shadows of the crypt, Diana realized that Comage had more than sized her up. He had gleaned her impressions, and in that respect was better acquainted with her than anyone else at Devereau House, except for Lucy.

Diana was encouraged by her own impressions. He was steady, open-minded, and trustworthy. He had a red neck, and he looked bucolic. Otherwise, he bore no resemblance to the widespread caricature of the piney-woods sheriff.

Diana paused a dozen feet from the mausoleum. "There are one or two things I didn't include back there at the house."

"I figured as much," he said. "Now's as good a time as any to get around to it."

He filled and lighted a rank looking old Wellington-curved pipe while Diana related all of it. Lucy's warning. The falling pitchfork. Cloty's suspicions. The break in the chapel wall behind the St. Joan niche. The discovery of the broken spectacles. Brief imprisonment in the crypt and the release by Fant. The disappearance of the spectacles.

He appeared phlegmatic and unperturbed throughout. When Diana had finished he nodded as if quietly turning a mental page. He knocked the dottle from the pipe, looked at the condition of the caking in the bowl, and thrust it in his pocket.

His eyes reflected the only physical sign that he'd heard Diana. They'd grown a fraction smaller, and Diana had the odd impression that he'd crouched down behind them.

This bloodhound wouldn't bay a warning, she thought, he would pounce. And an unwarranted little shiver traced her spine.

172

"Let's see the exact spot where you first saw those disappearing eye-glasses," he said.

It was but a short distance away, and when they reached it, Comage hunkered down with a heavy grunt.

He sat there for several seconds, forearms draped across his bent knees. His rounded back and shoulders were toward Diana. His hat moved slowly as his eyes searched.

He muttered an indistinct sound to himself. Then he eased out his right hand and began plucking away bits of brown pine needles.

"Well, how-do!" He lifted his palm to a point several inches below his mouth and gently blew away particles of vegetation.

Diana dropped to her knees beside him. "What is it, Mr. Comage?"

In answer, he extended his palm. Against its creases, sunlight caught against a small, thin piece of broken glass.

He rose up bearishly. "You said one lens was broken. We haven't got a regular eye doctor in the village. But we do have an old optometrist who fits glasses for the bayou folks and plantation workers. If he tells me this ain't a piece of glass from a lens, I'll change my name to Dum-dum!"

It was the most emotional statement he'd made. He pulled a handkerchief from his pocket and began enfolding the piece of glass. His fingers moved with an almost tender care, as if he'd been waiting a long time for this bit of glass.

He tucked the handkerchief in his shirt pocket, buttoning the flap. His crimped eyes strayed the remoteness of the swampland, and Diana could clearly pick up his thought. Where, in this vastness of turgid water and tangled jungle, was Cloty?

His sandpapery palm crunched on Diana's forearm. "Mind you, Miss Latham . . ." The thumb of his other hand stabbed his shirt pocket. "For now, this is between you and me. What you let from under your hat is out there for all the world to see."

Chapter 11

As Diana and Comage turned to go, they saw Philip striding from the direction of the house. With his tailoring and physical conditioning, he was the commanding figure of the successful young executive in the television commercials.

They met in the sun-dappled pathway. Philip's eyes glanced a question from his chiseled face, and Comage made a movement with his sloping shoulders that might have meant anything.

"I want something of Cloty's," Comage said. "Handkerchief, pair of stockings. Something to give some sharp-nosed hound dogs the scent."

"No problem," Philip said.

Comage flipped a thumb toward the swampland. "Too much out there for one man to search. It'll have to be done right. I'll organize half a dozen deputies in the village."

"Count me in," Philip said.

Comage shook his head. "I want a steady hand at the house. No reflections, Phil, but out there in the mangrove I'd prefer some red-necked trappers and fishermen."

Philip accepted the role with a wry grin. "It isn't as if I'd be a tenderfoot bother. I know those swamps almost as well as you do, Pierre. But all right, if that's the way you want it."

"You'll have a job to do keeping the house on an even keel—if Cloty doesn't turn up." Comage hitched his trousers. "I don't want anybody flying off the deep end. I want the lot of you to cool it and let the law do the job it gets paid for."

"Check," Philip said.

"Then I'll get things moving." With a brief nod of leave taking for Diana, Comage moved off. His gait was that of an awkward gorilla, but it carried him beyond the trees with astonishing rapidity.

Diana was very aware of Philip's presence beside her as they started the return walk to the house. Neither said anything immediately. Diana was still rankling from Robin's insinuations and accusations. She slipped a glance at Philip's rugged profile. She could take Robin in stride. Robin had her motives, and her methods. But what about Philip and Tony? Did they share any of Robin's views of the stranger in their midst?

Philip drew up, reaching for her hand. She swung about in the firmness of his grip.

"I don't blame you," he murmured.

"For what?"

"Feeling put out. Robin did get a little rough on you. It's the Cajun way, Diana. Pop off steam. Sing and dance at high noon if you feel like it. Blow your mind if the mood demands it."

"You don't have to apologize for her, Philip."

"I'm not. Robin is Robin, and there's much about her to appreciate."

"I'm sure of it. Would you like to go and appreciate her, Philip?"

He boomed a laugh. "See what I mean? It's catching. You're sounding like a Cajun vixen already."

Then as quickly as he'd laughed, he sobered. His arms swept her close. "Right now it's you I'm appreciating."

"Even if I'm not Diana Latham but a plotter in disguise?"

"Nonsense." His lips were parted to say more, but his eyes were rapt on her face. His eyes held her, and she was pleasantly warmed, imprisoned with him by the bars of sunlight that filtered down through the trees.

His lips touched hers in a lingering kiss. She felt the beating of her heart, and of his. Two hearts, racing in tempo.

Then she broke his lips away and tucked her cheek against his chest. "Philip . . ." she whispered, a small break in her voice.

"I know," he said gently, refusing to yield her during a final moment longer.

And he did know, she thought. They shared a sense of the shadows between them, the thoughts of Robin, the image of a shattered St. Joan statue, the silences unbroken by the sound of Cloty's voice.

"Perhaps the time will come for talking, Philip."

"I'm patient," he said. His arms slipped away slowly. He kissed her softly on the forehead, and he smiled. "Didn't I ever tell you that patience is one of my many virtues?"

They walked back to the house without meeting anyone, and he stood in the great hall watching her ascend the sweep of the stairway. She paused in the upper gallery before she entered her room, looking down at his lifted face. He blew her a kiss. She smiled in return, moving on then and entering her suite.

Closing the door, she slumped a little. Here in the quiet of her bedroom, she noticed how tired she was, how the past hours had filed away at her spirits and strength.

She walked slowly to the windows and looked at the primitive reaches of the landscape. Miles of mangrove tangle. Palmetto hummocks. Swaying seas of green sawgrass. Cottonmouths, alligators, swarming insects that could sting a person to madness, and a few roaming panthers. And twining through it all were the endless skeins of the swamp, a pattern of black water so treacherous the outlander could lose himself within a hundred yards of any starting point.

She thought how it would be in the hours to come. Lanky, weather-beaten men slipping across the skin of the swamp in water sleds, experienced eyes alert to every turning of a leaf and tremor of a twig. Comage moving in ever-widening circles, his bloodhounds in leash.

And if they don't find Cloty by nightfall, Diana thought, some of the men will return while others, impervious to the roiling masses of mosquitoes, will bed down on a spongy hummock. They will all start again tomorrow morning—when hope will have become as grayed as the first whisper of dawn.

It was a subdued group that finally gathered at dinner. Mrs. Lafarge had prepared a veal creole and a whipped yam dish as light and frothy as sea foam, but the beauty of the damask and silver appointed table was too dampened by the emptiness of Cloty's chair.

Huxley slumped at the head of the table with a mummified stillness, living in memories apparently more real than the present moment. Tony's attention was quickened by every small sound in the house that might herald news of Cloty.

Philip was the only one to display a calm appetite, complimenting Mrs. Lafarge as the courses were served. Wearing dark blue, Robin was a model in fine ivory with her wheaten hair worn in a chignon. She spoke little, but now and then, when she knew one of the others would notice, she glanced at Diana with eyes that seemed to say: No question now that something happened to Cloty; only question—how were you involved, Diana?

It was a stifling experience, made the more so when Comage dropped in with discouragingly little to report. His deputies, he said, would pick up the search tomorrow from their present locations. Yes, of course he had ferreted out Ozar Fant.

Comage reported that the old swamp squatter's story was simple: Fant claimed he was innocently on his way to his shack when he heard Diana screaming in the crypt. He had released her, told her she should "git from this place", and gone on about his business.

"Haven't a speck of evidence against him," Comage said. "Fact is, the evidence favors Ozar Fant. Wouldn't seem likely that he'd lock Miss Latham in the mausoleum only to hang around and let her out later. 'Course I could drum the broken-faced old cuss in on a charge of trespassing. I wouldn't be surprised if he's living on gleanings pilfered from Devereau plantation. Don't know as I could hold him long—but you want him jailed, Mr. Devereau?"

Huxley stirred, pushing a cup of untouched,

cold coffee aside and folding his thin, blue-veined hands on the table. "To what purpose?" he said.

"None, I guess," Comage said.

"He's an old man," Huxley said. "Let him have his living."

Comage nodded, rising from Cloty's chair, which he'd occupied while talking and having a cup of coffee. "I'll be in touch."

"Surely you'll find Cloty," Diana burst out. "A person doesn't vanish into thin air."

They looked at her slowly, with Cajun eyes. And she knew their meaning. The swamplands weren't thin air; out there, a hundred Clotys could vanish in a single trackless mile of boggy quicksands and scavengers.

A sense of unreal suspension slipped through Diana. Did one of the faces turned toward her mask the knowledge of what had really happened to Cloty . . . and to Lucy?

Comage broke the moment with a clearing of his throat. "Should Cloty turn up or you folks learn anything, call my office. The deputy on duty will fetch me by walkie-talkie."

The silent gathering broke up shortly after Comage departed. Avoiding both Philip and Tony, Diana went upstairs. She checked by Lucy's room and the nurse who relieved Abernathy said that Lucy was catnapping.

Going on to her room, Diana thought: Lucy is

181

going to note Cloty's absence. How can we tell Lucy the truth?

The next morning, Diana was impelled by pressures from two different sources. She could endure the vacuum of helpless waiting no longer, and she was ridden by questions that had come to her during the night, questions for Domina . . .

Wearing slacks, blouse, and sturdy laced oxfords, she strolled unobtrusively from the house after a scanty breakfast with Mrs. Lafarge in the kitchen.

Her primary destination was the stables, where she saddled and mounted the saucy pinto. The horse was skittish, eager to move. Diana curbed him with a knee and the reins. She looked over her shoulder, studying the house. It was a still-life from another era flanked by its towering chimneys and garnished with magnolias and poinsettias.

Diana shook aside the feeling that she was being watched, and let the pinto canter away from the stables.

Already the brilliant morning held a promise of crackling heat. The sky was an empty, cloudless glare. Gnats swirled in small black drifting clots over stagnant pools where dragonflies darted.

Diana chose the route she and Philip had followed, easily remembered. One by one the landmarks slipped by, a cane field, a fence, the giant curls of a cypress trunk that lightning had cloven in the distant past.

The scene crawled into view, the blood-red cottage beside the lagoon where the single-masted sailing skiff was tied up at the small pier.

Diana slipped from the pinto, hitching the horse to the base of a sapling near the front gate. Thick clumps of grass were within his range, and the pinto could browse the rest contentedly.

Crossing the tree-shaded yard, Diana watched for some sign of life. The small foreign car with the white canvas top was parked in the attached garage, but nothing moved in the breathless stillness.

Then the front doorway of the cottage framed the woman, Domina. She seemed to have materialized.

She wore a long garment of green silk with a choker collar and a headband of white. Her dark, handsome face was grave. Her large, expressive eyes reflected a remote kindness. Her robe rustled and draped her arm as she extended a hand toward Diana.

"Good morning, Diana. I knew you would come. I have a cold pitcher of bitteroot tea ready. The first taste is a bit acrid, but nothing on earth quenches a thirst quite so well."

Domina stepped aside, and Diana entered the bright, gay decor of the living room. She paused uncertainly near the middle of the pale green shag rug.

"You knew I would come?" Diana said. It must

be true. On the cocktail table was the tray Domina had already set out, a moisture-beaded silver pitcher, two glasses wearing knitted coasters like socklets, two tiny napkins, and a small array of pink-frosted confections.

"Should I claim psychic powers?" Domina asked. "It's a moment in which I might do so convincingly."

The ageless beauty of her Egyptian-like face admitted a smile. "The truth is, I put several things together and strongly suspected you would come."

She raised a loosely closed hand and flicked open, one by one, fingers ringed with emerald and topaz as she ticked off: "You were delighted by the cottage and fascinated by its denizen on your previous visit, boding for a return out of curiosity, if nothing else. Burdened by the heavy hours since the disappearance of Clotilde Mathis you had to get away for a little time, and this is the only other place you know. The questions I saw in your eyes when you came with Philip are now burning for answers. The . . ."

"Enough," Diana said with a strained laugh. "You've read me like a first-grade introduction to the alphabet."

"And lastly," Domina added confidentially, "I glimpsed you on the pinto across the lagoon. I had already made the tea, and it gave me time to prepare the tray. In any event, I'm glad I don't have to drink my potion alone. Please sit down, Diana."

184

Diana sank on the white sailcloth couch. Domina sat down on a matching chair she had placed to face the couch, the cocktail table between.

Domina picked up the pitcher and poured, her every movement graceful. She could cross a room and make it a quiet ballet, Diana thought.

"You mentioned Cloty's disappearance," Diana said.

"And you're wondering how I knew. Nothing mysterious about it, Diana. Word of everything that happens in the parish trickles to me quickly. Sometimes I'm able to help."

She handed an icy glass to Diana. "But this time —no. If any of my people knew anything about it I would have fetched Cloty back to Devereau House already."

Diana sank back. One of the questions that had risen in the darkness of her restless night was gnawing through her. It was an intuition drawn from little things, the old portrait of a girl of amoral and devilish beauty, Huxley Devereau's unexpected and shocking reaction to the mere mention of the girl's name.

Prospera Clantell.

The name was so meaningful that it had been stricken out, buried in the past of Devereau House.

"Who was she, Domina?"

"She?"

"Prospera Clantell."

Domina's composed, regal face showed nothing, except in the eyes. Diana didn't miss the inner twitch.

"Why should I tell you anything about Prospera Clantell, Diana?"

"I'll get it somehow—and in view of your regard for Huxley, I think you'd prefer to be the source."

"You make a truly strong point, Diana."

"The choice is up to you."

"But have you left me with one?" Domina asked. She set her glass down slowly. Folding her ringed fingers in her lap, she sat with the impassiveness of a Delphian oracle.

"Prospera Clantell was a brief and tragic chapter in Huxley's life many years ago," Domina said. "He was an exuberant young man, high-spirited, dashing, reckless. Born in the wrong time. He belonged to another page of history, among the king's musketeers or in command of an Elizabethan ship ransacking Spanish galleons. As happens to high-born young men on occasion, Huxley's temperament failed to note sufficient challenge and excitement in his surroundings—until something happened to change him. He spent his energies—squandered them, I should say—in the fastest New Orleans circles, drinking, gambling, indulging wild whims."

Domina paused, then said, "I don't excuse Huxley. I explain him for your understanding. There is much in him, has always been, that's admirable."

"I think so, too," Diana nodded.

"He met and married a beautiful woman, Maria DuVal. He loved her devotedly. She was the perfect mistress of Devereau House, gracious, sensitive. Their first child, Tony, was born, and two years later a darling of a girl, Lucy. They seemed the perfect family, the enviable ideal, blessed with everything. But perhaps even utopia palls and grows monotonous—and in a period of restlessness Huxley met Prospera Clantell."

Domina stopped, and the silence was jarring. A bleak smile impinged the strong mouth. "Do you understand, my dear?"

"Yes," Diana said, looking away.

"Prospera Clantell was everything his wife was not, cheap, vulgar, greedy. Yes, a greedy spitfire. Huxley loathed himself even in the time of their passion. But he was like a man drugged, drawn to a fire of evil."

Domina's eyes lifted to a point in space and time, lingered, lowered, slowly closed. "The ending is as old as the history of human beings trapped by their own foolish acts. Prospera secretly summoned Huxley to her bayou shanty. She told Huxley she was carrying his child and requested a great deal of money. He turned to go, and she attacked him with a knife. He shoved her in a sprawl and departed. He didn't know right then that what she had said was true, or that he had injured her."

Domina's eyelids lifted, veils slipping from deeply shadowed pools.

"Alone and in agony, Prospera lost more than the child that day. The mind that had always tettered on the brink between sanity and savagery flipped over the edge. She came to Devereau House with the obsession to make Huxley pay. She had an old revolver. She saw him near the stables. She walked up and started shooting, continuing until the gun was empty. One of the bullets shattered his hipbone, marking him for a lifetime with a limp . . . a token reminder . . ."

"Did they catch her?"

"Of course they caught her, Diana. Off in the swamps. Bedraggled, with burning eyes, she was. Sitting cross-legged on a hummock and making little voodoo dolls out of shredded palmetto fronds. And laughing. Laughing all the while. Laughing wild threats even as they quietly shipped her off to an asylum at the other end of the state. Yes, Prospera Clantell was caught."

"And Huxley's wife . . . Lucy's and Tony's mother . . ." Diana said. "Maria DuVal drove away from Devereau House and was killed in the smashup of her car."

"Killed when she learned the truth, Diana, that

sent her in headlong flight away from Devereau House."

Diana eased against the back of the couch. She felt powerless to look away from Domina's face. How well this woman had hid her own regrets and disappointments. How often she must have yearned for more from Huxley than friendship, for the encirclement of his arms, the fire of his lips, the sharing of his name.

"You are wise, Diana. You are intuitive," Domina said softly. "You sense my secret, I think."

"I believe I know now why you've stayed here on the lagoon all these years, close to Devereau House, when you might have traveled the world," Diana said.

"You must never put it in words, but out of your mind."

"But why haven't you told Huxley, shown him how you really felt?"

"Ah," it was a thin sigh, "in that you are not so wise, Diana. I would rather have his friendship than nothing. After Prospera Clantell and Maria DuVal, he knew fears and obsessions of his own. He dares admit no woman past the line of friendship. It is a fact of life, a result of life. If I tried to change him, I would lose what I have of him."

Without visibly changing, Domina seemed different. A welling sympathy for the woman thickened Diana's throat. "I think," she laughed shakily, "that you're too good for Huxley Devereau or most any other man."

"And that," Domina said drily, "is the very first thing I would change, if I had the power to dictate my birth."

A stillness came, fraught with the things Domina had revealed.

"Victims of ourselves," Domina murmured. "Myself, Huxley, Maria DuVal, Prospera Clantell. Even Fant."

Diana's brows lifted. "Ozar Fant?"

"Capable of love, like the rest of us," Domina said. "A generation ago he was a gaunt young simpleton, unable to get beyond the third grade. A back-bayou nobody. A nothing, compared to Huxley Devereau. But Fant worshipped Prospera Clantell. He withdrew further into the swamps after she was taken away, became almost a recluse. He would save his money, penny by penny, put on his red-gallused finest, and buy a bus ticket."

"To the further end of the state," Diana said.

Domina nodded. "To visit the woman he never stopped adoring. I suspect he was the only visitor Prospera Clantell ever had. He was faithful, throughout the years. Finally, he was old, and the hardships of the swamps were too much. He ventured back to the edges of civilization."

"Does he still make the trips to the asylum?"

"Oh, no. A few months ago, he returned with

190

his spirits dragging and mentioned to a store-keeper in the village that Prospera Clantell had died, old and forgotten. She was buried, Fant said, in a pauper's grave. Someday, he promised, he would buy a little marker."

The gloom of it all, the tragedy and waste, coiled through Diana like a tendril of chill swamp fog. Then she got up stiffly. "I hope our next visit will be in a lighter vein."

Domina walked with her to the door. "Then you will come again?"

"If I may."

A patient smile humanized Domina's austere face. "You were welcome before. Now you are even more so, knowing us for what we are and accepting us."

"Thank you, Domina." She hurried from the house, lifting her hand in a small farewell wave when she was halfway across the yard.

She untied the pinto and swung lithely into the saddle.

Riding back to Devereau House, she went over everything she'd seen and heard from the moment of her arrival. She was nagged with the certainty that Domina had told her even more than either of them realized.

Chapter 12

When she entered the house, Diana hurried to the upper gallery. She was conscious of the stillness. The silence was like a held breath. With a little effort of the imagination, the house had a creature awareness, a patient waiting for its own dark purposes to be worked out.

Diana paused at the door of Lucy's room, composing herself and regaining her breath from the rapid climb up the main stairway.

She tapped lightly with her fingertips, and Abernathy responded, opening the door.

Abernathy nodded, murmuring "Miss Latham" in greeting.

"How is Lucy?" Diana asked.

Abernathy's long, homely face yielded a smile, showing square horsey teeth. "The doctor might have prescribed you earlier." She stroked her heavy chin, studying Diana. "I can't tell whether

Lucy is mainly glad or worried that you're here. Maybe both. But whatever, it's got her making new demands on herself to keep on living."

A movement of Abernathy's starched green uniform unblocked the doorway. Diana entered the barrenly antiseptic room, moving to the side of the hospital bed.

Abernathy was right. Lucy's color was the nearest normal today that Diana had seen it. Her quick dark eyes were almost as they had been when the going got rough in Iaxtaca. Not happy eyes. But eyes beginning to glint with scorn at the thought of ultimate defeat.

While the nurse busied herself toying with instruments at the stainless steel sterilizer, Diana smiled down at Lucy and opened with small talk, about the friskiness of the pinto, the drowsiness of the hot day.

Lucy blinked an ireful little message of impatience.

"Okay," Diana said. "So what's the question?" She rested Lucy's hand in her palm and started intoning the alphabet. Lucy's finger stopped her at "C" and, the second time through, at "L".

"C-l . . ." Diana said. "Cloty?"

Lucy blinked. Yes.

"You're wondering why Cloty hasn't been in?"
Yes.

Diana was aware of Abernathy's abrupt cessation of motion at the sterilizer. How long can we keep it from Lucy? Diana thought. Long enough to get Cloty back?

Before her hesitancy could stretch out noticeably, Diana said, "Didn't Cloty mention she was going into the village?"

"Dang me," Abernathy broke in, quick on the uptake, "I didn't tell Lucy. She was napping the last time Cloty looked in."

Diana felt a twinge of guilt at the way they were stretching the truth. But it seemed to satisfy Lucy for the time being.

Diana eased her hand free. "Now," she said as lightly as she could manage, "I have a question of my own."

Fire away, Lucy's eyes instructed.

"Let's go back to the day of the accident," Diana said, "once more."

Lucy's eyes agreed, bright, expectant.

"The last time we talked," Diana said, "I was so anxious to find out what had happened at the chapel that I couldn't think of anything else. But now I want to go back a little further. It's the day of the accident, but you haven't yet left the house."

I understand, Lucy's eyes said.

Across the room, Abernathy had grown quiet, cautiously closing the sterilizer. Just don't interfere, Diana thought without looking at the nurse.

"You decide to go to the chapel," Diana said to Lucy. "Now you are leaving the house, crossing the patio. Was anyone out there?"

194

Lucy blinked twice. No.

"Okay." Diana leaned closer to the bed. "You pass by the swimming pool, the garage. See anyone yet?"

No.

Diana felt Abernathy's presence drifting close. "What's this?" the nurse murmured. "I don't like the rise of color in her cheeks, Miss Latham."

Diana's forearm slipped out to ease Abernathy back. For once, she felt herself Abernathy's equal in plain brute strength.

"The garage falls behind and you're approaching the path, the woods, Lucy," Diana pressed on. "Do you see him now?"

Yes. Quickly.

"Did you speak?"

No.

"You just happened to glimpse him as he hurried off through the woods?"

Yes.

"Then you lost sight of him?"

Yes.

"Did you see him again?"

No.

"You'd seen him around the place before, every now and then."

Yes.

"So seeing him that day didn't seem important, and you continued on toward the chapel, quickly dismissing the thought of him, your mind crowded with other things."

Lucy signaled a yes. That's the way it was, Diana. And the great dark eyes smoldered a question: How important was it, Diana?

"You arrived at the chapel without seeing anyone else?" Diana asked.

Yes.

Diana straightened, pulling her body from its hovering attitude. We've closed the gap, she thought. We're opening the scene we covered in our last talk. Lucy in the chapel. The silence broken by a little animal rustling outside. Lucy looking up, seeing the St. Joan rushing down upon her . . .

Diana heard the sibilance of Abernathy's breathing close beside her. The nurse, for an instant, was helpless in a net of curiosity.

"Who are you talking about, Miss Latham? Who was it Lucy glimpsed out there that day before she reached the chapel?"

Instead of answering directly, Diana spoke to Lucy: "Are we talking about the same man? Ozar Fant?"

Lucy blinked. Yes, we are talking about the same man.

Abernathy humphed. She was disappointed that it was only Fant whom Lucy'd seen. "That old chicken thief should have been locked up weeks ago for trespassing."

"But he wasn't," Diana said.

"Well, my imagination won't stretch a connection between the old rummy and Lucy's accident." Abernathy's solid form was bumping Diana aside. "And I think you'd best go now. Time to get some nourishment into our patient."

Diana was ready to accept the dismissal. She gave Lucy's hand a brief squeeze and added a smile. "See you later."

Lucy's eyes followed her across the room. Diana turned at the doorway for a backward glance. Abernathy was readying an intravenous feeding.

With a goodbye wink at Lucy, Diana went out. Her movements quickened in the hallway. Almost brushing the bannister, she looked into the grand hall below, struck by its emptiness. Where had everyone gone?

She descended the main stairway at a rapid clip. She stood hesitant, the corner of her lip caught between her teeth. She longed for the sight of Philip. It would take a man's strength to beard Ozar Fant.

She thought of trying to get in touch with Constable Comage. But it might take hours before he could be reached, break off his search, and arrive at Devereau House. Diana was afraid to waste so much time. If her suspicions of Fant were true, too much time had passed already.

Muffled sounds drifted from the back part of

197

the house, snapping Diana's head up. She hurried through the hall, across the dining room, and into the kitchen.

Three of the servants were there. The Lafarges had evidently returned from marketing. The pleasant, easygoing manservant was carrying in large brown bags of groceries. His wife, the cook, was cursorily checking each bag as he set it on the table and instructing Myree how to arrange the items in the pantry.

All three glanced about. Lafarge was the first to note the tightness in Diana's face. He slipped a well-packed supermarket bag onto the kitchen table.

"Why, Miss Latham . . . Anything wrong? News of Cloty?"

"No," Diana shook her head, "I haven't heard a thing. I was looking for Mr. Lockridge."

Mrs. Lafarge was taking a long old-fashioned pin from her sensible, sun-shading straw hat. "I think he and Miss Robin and Mr. Huxley drove off together just before Mr. Lafarge and me left in the station wagon."

"Oh. I see. Do you know where they went?"

"Just one supermarket in the village, serves the whole parish," the manservant said. "On our way, I saw Mr. Lockridge's car parked near the constable's office. I guess they were in there to get some action in the search for Cloty."

Myree had resumed her work, and was in the

198

pantry clattering canned goods. "Mr. Tony was through here a minute ago," she called. "Been off in the swamps since early day, I reckon, for all the good it done. Looked tuckered. You might find him out back."

"Thank you, Myree." Diana rushed on through the kitchen, leaving the Lafarges staring after her.

She saw Tony when she stepped onto the patio. He was seated at a table near the swimming pool, sipping ice water from a tall glass. The sun etched his profile. He was wan, and boyishly vulnerable. He sat looking into distant spaces, his lean shoulders burdened.

He wasn't a proud princeling of Devereau House, but common clay with inner questions that went to the heart of life and living. Suffering a little, because he would, unlike Philip, never have all the answers.

Diana had never witnessed him in a moment so unguarded. A bitter sweetness came to her throat. She was urged to go to him, to touch him, to share his embrace.

But before she moved, she coughed, giving him an awareness of her presence and chance to collect himself as she crossed over to him.

Startled from his reverie, he got up quickly and pulled out the wrought-iron chair next to his. She didn't accept it, but stood facing him.

She was troubled by a question. She felt a warmth and tenderness for Tony that Philip didn't need. Philip warmed her in a different way, with his steadiness and strength. The next hour, and the action she had in mind, required steadiness. Tony had his own kind of strenght. But he was mercurial. Could she count on him?

Her indecision brought a frown to Tony's gaunt face. "What is it, Diana?"

"I haven't seen you around today," she said, stalling.

He was dressed in faded jeans and a knitted shirt strained tight against his chest and forearms. The garments were blackened in places with perspiration. "No, I was up and out like the great white hunter," he said.

He ran his hand through the shagginess of his black hair. "I used to be pretty good in the swamps, when I was a kid tracking and observing the small creatures that interested me. Thought I might pick up a spoor. Started out where you found Cloty's broken eyeglasses. The only sign I cut," he grinned in self-disparagement, "was my own."

"I was busy myself, Tony. I rode over to Domina's. I . . . ." She wanted to drop her eyes away, but she looked at him in candor. "I know the story of your father and Prospera Clantell."

A fuse sputtered in his eyes. The corner of his mouth jerked. "So now what do you make of us?"

"I make you people, Tony. I make you part of

the human race, that always seems to pay so dearly for its mistakes."

He moved his hand slowly, touching her cheek. The hackles relaxed. He quit standing there as if he were at bay. "You would," he said.

"And I know the other part—about Ozar Fant and his simple-minded lifelong devotion to Prospera Clantell."

Tony's hand dropped away. "Fant had his religion. Not a tree to worship, or an idol or amulet. Its name was Prospera Clantell. He had his mecca, the place where she was. He made his pilgrimages."

And the guilty conscience in Devereau House let him scrounge a sneaky living off the plantation, Diana thought, feeling it owed Fant that much.

Diana slipped a look at the house and driveway. Still no sign of Philip. There was only Tony.

Diana moistened her lips. "I just now learned something more about Ozar Fant from Lucy. She passed him in the woods, minutes before she was crushed by the statue."

Muscles ridged in Tony's jaw. He searched Diana's face for any sign of uncertainty.

"Tony, if someone wanted to destroy Devereau House," Diana said in a breaking voice, "what better tool than Ozar Fant? He's hated this house for a lifetime. If someone offered him money and cleverly worked on Fant's desire for revenge, who knows what the old man would do?"

"Dear God," Tony whispered. Grains of moisture shone on his forehead. "Fant was out there the day Lucy . . ." He choked off.

"And at the mausoleum after I was locked in," Diana said. "And when he disappeared from there so did Cloty's broken eyeglasses."

Tony's eyes were blazing, his hands working, opening, closing. He quivered with a single thought. "Fant watching . . . seeing Lucy enter the chapel . . . the dirty old devil!"

"Tony . . ." Diana caught his arm. His bicep was bunched to rock hardness.

He punched her touch aside. "Leave me alone, Diana. His neck is overdue for a wringing. Comage let him off the hook too easily, hung up like everybody else with the idea of Fant as a harmless old swamp eccentric."

Tony started to move around her. Diana stumbled back, barring the way.

"Cool it, Tony!"

He thrust out his arm, pressing her aside. The quick movement of his sandals made dry, rasping sounds. Diana ran a few steps to catch up with him. She had to take three steps to his two to match his long stride.

"Tony . . ."

"Cut out, Diana. I'll take care of Fant."

She looked over her shoulder, yearning for the sight of Philip, Huxley, or even the manservant Lafarge.

202

Gasping, she stayed at Tony's side. "I'll just bet you will," she said, her voice throaty with anger. "And if Fant knows anything about Cloty, I wouldn't be surprised if you broke his mouth before he could tell it!"

He cut her with a dark look. "So I'm the hotheaded kid on the schoolground?"

"You're giving a good imitation."

He quickened his pace another notch, his destination the stables. "If you think I can't handle Fant—and do it right—why don't you go get Philip? He knows the location of Fant's shack as well as I do."

"Oh, you . . . !" Diana burst out helplessly, struggling to keep up with him.

Ignoring her, he was in and out of the tack room, a saddle slung across his shoulder. He stopped at the third stall along the row. A chestnut horse arched its neck over the low gate, shook its beautiful mane, and pawed with an eager forehoof.

Tony lifted a bridle from its hook beside the gate. Hesitating, he turned and spoke, his voice reaching Diana as she was about to enter the tack room.

"Planning to chaperone me?"

"Something like that."

"Fant may turn out to be dangerous."

"Yes, he might," she said, gripping the rough door jamb.

"Can't I scare you off?"

"No," she said.

"Talk you out of it?"

"No."

"You're as flipped out as I am."

"Maybe I am, Tony."

"Then get a move on," he said. "Maybe the horses will show some sense."

Chaper 13

Fant's place was closer than Diana expected. She'd imagined him in the swamp's vastness, although she remembered what Domina had said about Fant moving closer to civilization when the years had worn him down, stiffening once tireless limbs and dulling the edge of falcon-sharp eyes.

Tony set out in an easterly direction, following a narrow trail through the cane fields. Diana imagined it was the route for chugging loaded trucks at harvest time.

The pinto was ready after his rest, and Diana swept along with Tony over a mile-long swale of sawgrass that undulated in the breeze like the young wheat fields of Kansas.

The shadows of a pine forest folded over them. Tony rode without the niceties of horsemanship that Philip displayed. In the saddle, Tony abandoned himself to the horse and became a part of it.

The trail narrowed, and Diana gave Tony the lead. They slowed as the forest thickened, ducking now and then to avoid low hanging branches.

Tony drew up in a small glen where sunlight and shade threw a polka dot pattern.

Tony slid from the saddle. "We'll tether the horses here. Fant's shack is just beyond those thickets."

He hitched the horses to a drooping pine bough, slapped a determined mosquito from his cheek, and motioned with his head. "Easy does it now. As little noise as you can make. Like a pair of TV Indians."

He padded forward, and the underbrush swallowed him. Diana hurried in his wake, ignoring brambles and slashing vines, keeping flickers of Tony's figure in sight through breaks ahead. Her heart lurched as he vanished and she thought she'd lost him. She clambered over a huge fallen pine trunk that was pulpy with rot and working with grubs.

Crouching and shielding her head with her arms, she pressed through a tangle of vines. She thrust out her hand to part a gossamer gray curtain of hanging panish moss, and almost stumbled into Tony. Bent low, he had halted at the edge of a wild cane-break.

He drew Diana down beside him. Disheveled and damp from exertion, they crowded together. The earth was mucky underfoot, the air brittle

206

with heat, smelling of turgid water and riotous vegetation.

"We're on the edges of the bayou," Tony said. "Fant's house is less than a hundred yards away. I'll scout the place. If I whistle once, come on in. If twice—run like crazy, mount up, and ride as if the devil were at your heels. He just might be."

"Tony . . ." Her voice dropped away.

"What is it, Diana?"

"Be careful, Tony."

"Goes without saying, old pal of mine. Sorry you came?"

"Of course not. Just a few butterflies inside, that's all."

Looking at her, his eyes crinkled. "Know something? You're as mussed, rumpled, wind-blown, and grubby as a Cajun woman after a day of helping her husband at his traplines."

She hadn't a ready retort. One thing about him, you never knew what he would think or say in a given time or place.

He made a small movement, brushing her lips with his.

"And you're beautiful," he said.

"Tony, you're impossible."

"I know. And you're sweet. And I hope that Fant, if he's home, is in a tractable mood."

He stood up and swished through the cane-break. Diana waited, holding her breath. Tony's short, crisp whistle came to her, a single time.

She came out of the underbrush into a clearing shaded by spreading live oaks. The bayou opened out before her like an irregular blue scar in the jungle. Fant's house stood several yards from the water's edge. It was a one-room pine-slab and tar-paper shanty sagging on its foundation of short, stilt-like posts.

Tony was standing a few feet from the corner of the house, holding out his hand and motioning Diana on.

"Fant doesn't seem to be about," he said when Diana reached his side. "Come on. We'll do a little genteel snooping while we have the chance."

They rounded the corner to the side of the shack facing the bayou. The front door, narrow and weathered, was crudely tacked together from old packing crate scraps. It hung on strap hinges cut from junked automobile tires and was secured by a tattered loop of rope hooked about a rusty nail.

Tony slipped the loop, pushed the door open, and offered a steadying hand on her elbow as Diana hoisted herself inside with a single high step.

Diana blinked against the suffocatingly dim interior. Two small, glassless windows on either side were hung with limp burlap. A little light filtered in, but no air.

Tony crowded beside her. They looked over the shanty in silence. A pang of disappointment went through Diana. No place here to conceal Cloty—if it had been Fant who'd taken her. Just the evidences of Fant's scanty life: A sway-backed cot, a rusty kerosene stove, a rickety table holding a lantern, water bucket, tin basin, and a few cracked dishes. His spare overalls and denim shirt hung on a nail in the futher corner, near the cot.

Diana's roving gaze stopped, returned to a shelf bracketed on the rear wall. It was made from a fresh piece of planking, about four feet long, thrusting out from the wall a dozen inches. On it stood a pair of tall white candles and half a dozen photographs in dime store frames.

Drawing closer, Diana saw a grimy, dog-eared ringed notebook lying between the candles.

She picked up the largest of the pictures, turning it to catch the feeble light. Cracked and faded, the young girl image was dressed in the long-skirted style of forty years ago. Framed in sausage curls, her smiling face was tilted pertly. It was the same vulgar prettiness that Domina had caught on one of her earliest canvases, Diana thought.

"Tony," she said.

He was already beside her, lowering his shoulders to peer at the pictures one by one.

"Prospera Clantell . . . all of them of Prospera Clantell when she was young and life was a future," his murmur was bleak, "a promise for all of them."

All of them, Diana thought, a future including

209

Fant and the girl, Tony's own father and mother, death and a madhouse, Lucy and a St. Joan statue, and Tony and me standing here in this moment . . .

"Fant had his idol, his mecca—and now we see his shrine, with candles to light his icons," Tony said heavily. "I wonder if this is his liturgy?"

He lighted a candle with a paper match and carefully opened the brittle pages of the notebook.

Head close to Tony's, Diana tried to make out the painful writing efforts of a man close to illiteracy. Misspelled and crudely formed, the blurred penciled words sometimes stood alone, evoking a thought and memory known to Fant, substituting for a complete sentence.

The first entry was dated thirty-nine years ago, almost to the day:

"Oh, Lord, hev mersy. She shot D. Doan keer fer him. But Prospera . . . my Prospera . . . they'll ast yore life."

Diana hardly breathed as the crude diary moved on through the years, often with long blanks.

"There is mersy. Her life spared. But she bin tooken away. Heered corthouse talk. She tooken to crazy house. Wisht I wuz ded. Put pistol to my hed, but firin pin didnt wurk. She gone. I caint go. It is a sign."

"Went to asilum. Wouldnt let me see her. Sed come back in months."

"Bin trappin all winter. Bowt blue surge suit and bus fare. They let me see her. She doant no me."

"Winter agin. Lonesum. Just her pixure to talk to."

"Asilum folks nice. Let me see her. She knowed me. Glory!"

"Another winter and I hev seen her. She knowed me and kin talk good. She kin recolleck. But they wont let her go. Sed she wont ever go. Sed she is dangerous. Sed she is homey-sidal."

The faithful visits continued as the seasons and years fled. Then: "Laid up, bad. Wuz killin gators for skins. Feller buys them for shoe factury. Best muney I ever dun made. But big bull gator stove in my fase with his tale. Liken to dyed. Lived. But laid up long time. Seen myself in lookin glass. And I cryed."

"Caint hev her see me the way I look. Wont go back. Fase hurts a lot, but not like my hart."

"Tuff winter. Thawt much. If I dont go, who will? Bin nigh twenty yrs. since they tooken her. Never staid away so long. She think I am ded. Will go, fase an all."

"She kissed my fase. Then sed D done it. She wood fix D. She went wild. They stropped her up. Sed my visit was bad for her. It was my fase done it. My hart broke."

"Bad summer. Broke arm cuttin timber."

211

"Arm good, but stiff. Wrote them a letter, beggin to see her."

"I doant heer. Whut are they doin to her?"

"Went on bus. They let me see her. Good visit. Never fergit. Like me, she is gettin old. But still purty."

"Wet, cold winter. Come down with swamp fever. Liken to dyed. But it was good. In my franzy thought she wuz here with me. Two days an nites she with me til fever broke and noggin kleared. Am broke and caint buy bus ticket."

"Strength back. Worked road gang. Went to see her. Bad visit. She is tard of that place. Gettin older and tarder, like me."

The visits went on, affecting Fant's emotional state. When his Prospera was cheerful, he was happy, although suffering pains and illnesses of his encroaching years.

Tony turned the final page: "Wasted bus ticket. Rode all that way for nothin. They tole me. She is gone. Has this day come? My Prospera ain't there no more. D sits in his big house and reckons it all over. But I kin tell him better. They is them that wood like to skin you, Mr. D."

Tony's eyes were glued to the last line. Diana gently closed the bedraggled notebook, the means of bringing back memories to a simple-minded man who realized he would forget if he didn't write it down.

Tony lifted his face slowly. He was about to

speak, when Fant's nasal twang erupted in the doorway: "Folks from the big house always did have their nerve with other people's goods!"

Tony and Diana spun about. She choked back a small sound, clutching Tony's arm. The doorway framed Fant's rawboned, denim-clad figure, his hovering, misshapen face, the old shotgun he was gripping in both gnarled hands.

He took one hand from the gun to grip the door post and haul himself up.

" 'Pears like the tables is turned, Devereau. Now it's you doing the poaching."

Tony edged himself partially between Diana and the old man. "We were waiting for you, Fant."

"I can bet. And sneaking a look in every cranny to pass the time while you waited, I reckon."

"We must talk to you, Mr. Fant," Diana said.

"I'm short on words today, little lady." Fant's weirdly arranged eyes stabbed about the shanty, trying to decide the extent of Tony's and Diana's search.

He sidled past the oil stove, halting with his rawboned form shielding the crockery cluttered table.

His right eye settled on Diana balefully. "I thought I told you once to git. I gave you the chance. How come," he complained, "you couldn't take an old man's honest advice?"

With the gun settled in the crook of his right

213

arm, he reached behind himself with his other hand. His fumbling brought a small clatter from the chipped crockery. His hand closed over an object. He picked it up, and as he slipped it into his hip pocket, Diana caught the glint of a delicate chain dripping from his fingers.

A neck chain—Cloty's eyeglasses!

But the gun was too real for Diana to find comfort in proof that Fant had taken the broken spectacles after he'd released her from the mausoleum.

He shuffled from the table, his muddy brogans scuffing sandpapery sounds from the gritty plank floor.

"You ought not to come here with him, little lady. What do you owe Devereau House?"

"Fant, you owe yourself something," Tony said.

"Yeah?"

"A thought of the trouble you're making for yourself."

"I swan," the old man said almost cordially, "now if that ain't just like a Devereau. You bust in my place, and it's me making the trouble!"

"The gun spells trouble, Fant."

"It do—for you."

"It's not too late to talk it over like reasonable men." Tony moved a step forward. The gun snapped up, its twin barrels yawning at his midsection.

"I reckon," Fant said, "I lost what little reason I had a long way back, Devereau. Now the time has come when I don't care. You follow me? You can't scare me, on account of I don't much care what happens to me anymore."

"But you're important, Mr. Fant," Diana burst out, "as important as any human being. You can't undo whatever you've done, but going on blindly won't help."

"You talk good, m'am. But that don't help either." Fant motioned a small command with the gun barrel. "I see you been reading my book. Laughing at the old pictures too, I reckon."

"No, Mr. Fant," Diana said. "There's nothing here to laugh at. Only to regret."

'I'm not begging for sympathy." Fant knuckled a hand across his twisted mouth. "Now you put the candle out, and git away from them things!"

Tony moved quietly, as if getting out of Diana's way. But he let the motion slip him closer to Fant's right side, and his eyes drilled a message that caused Diana's heart to lurch. He was asking for a split-second chance to jump Fant.

The candle flame wavered in her vision. No, Tony, don't take the chance . . .

But what other chance was there?

With a steadiness that surely couldn't belong to her, Diana snuffed out the candle and picked up Fant's diary.

"Put the book down, m'am!"

Diana's stomach was squeezing itself into a knot of thorny cactus. "It's a very interesting

215

book, Mr. Fant," she said, drifting toward the couch and widening the space between her and Tony.

"I'm not obliged for your opinion, little lady!" Fant's broken features were showing red. "The book ain't for your eyes!"

All but ignoring him, Diana idled on alongside the cot.

"Put the book down." Fant bit the words one by one, his right eye jutting.

"Very well, Mr. Fant."

Diana thrust the limp notebook toward him, and his reflex was automatic. He took a half step, reaching to snatch the diary from her hand. In the same instant, he caught the hint of Tony's movement from the corner of his eye. He spun, swinging the gun. The weapon slapped against Tony's palm.

The momentum and Tony's strength snapped the gun muzzle toward the roof. Tony closed with Fant, shouting, "Down, Diana"

She was dropping already, jellied with anticipation of the gun's blast. Her palms and knees struck the floor. Scrambling away, she heard the hard stomping of their feet, the smack of fists against flesh, their throaty sounds as they struggled for the gun.

She saw the savagery in Fant's face and wondered how Tony could stand up to it. Fant was kicking and gouging at Tony's face. Tony swung away and struck Fant with an uppercut. Fant staggered, and Tony wrung the gun loose, using both hands. Tony staggered under the force of his own wrenching weight. With a hoarse shout of fear, Fant hurled himself out through the open doorway.

Tony was after him in an instant, dropping to the ground and disappearing.

Diana ran to the door, her heart hammering. She fought off a suffocation, her eyes sweeping the bayou, the choking masses of vegetation. That quickly, they had vanished.

Chapter 14

A myriad of wild visions flashed through Diana's mind. Fant dropping from a low tree limb panther-like onto Tony's back. Fant coiled in a thicket, slithering out behind Tony. Fant striking with a stone or club and tearing the gun from Tony's hands . . .

She steadied her thoughts. It was no time to panic. Available help was too far away. If she threw discretion aside and yielded to the quixotic impulse to dash to Tony's assistance herself, she would get lost in the morass and perhaps offer the wily old man a hostage.

Regardless of her uncertainties, it was up to Tony, whether he or Fant came walking back in one piece.

She backed away from the door, searching quickly and finding a heavy old butcher knife on

Fant's table. Her nerveless fingers closed about the handle. The weapon felt awkward, ridiculous. It was frightful and unreal to be holding it. But she clung to it grimly as she ran to the door and dropped outside.

She felt better with space around her in which to dart and run. She stood in the yard with shoulders drawn, listening to the unabated hum of insect life. She was wary, watchful, attuned even to the rustle of Spanish moss veiling the trees.

She snapped around as the breaking of a weed initiated a threshing in a drab, brown thicket.

She backed slowly, watching the rattling movement in the cat-tails and reeds. She tried to hold the knife with menace, hoping the bluff would give her time to break for the horses, if it should be Fant who broke into the clearing.

She listened to him slogging steadily across the marshy isthmus that thumbed into the bayou. She caught glimpses of him, and a broken sound of relief welled in her throat.

She dropped the knife and ran to meet him as Tony broke out of the foliage. He was muck-stained to his knees, unkempt from his exertions, rivulets of perspiration coursing down his bramble-scratched cheeks. He was still carrying Fant's shotgun, dangling tiredly from his right hand.

"Tony . . ."

She pressed her arms about him, content for the

219

moment with the assurance of his unharmed presence.

He slipped his left arm about her waist. "I like the welcome," he grinned. "Maybe I'll duck off into the swamp every hour or so."

"Are you all right, Tony?"

"Like I'm just warming up for the main event."

They drew apart and started walking toward the shack. His mood became darkly serious. "Fant was just too slippery."

"You mustn't blame yourself, Tony."

"I can help it, a little, even knowing it would be tough for half a dozen men to corner the old boy in his own arena." He looked at the shotgun before shoving it through the open door of the shanty. "Maybe I should have slowed him down with a spray of birdshot. I had him in sight twice."

Diana's eyes dwelt on him. "I'm glad you don't find it easy to shoot off guns, Tony."

"I had every excuse."

"I know," she said. "I also saw him slip Cloty's glasses in his pocket. Tony, could he have . . . done away with her?"

"I'm not sure. It doesn't jibe with the man revealed in Fant's diary. However ignorant, he was born with rare patience and compassion."

"Does anything jibe?" Diana asked bleakly. "Cloty isn't here, that's for sure."

"It's the first place anyone would come looking for Fant and asking questions," Tony nodded, "consequently the last place even a dim-wit would stash a captive."

Diana drooped with defeat. "Where could she be, Tony?"

He grasped her hand. "Come on. I may have figured it out on my way back, after I lost Fant."

He explained while they hurried across the yard and into the wood. A fisherman had built and occupied the little house years ago, moving on after choking algae turned the bayou into a dying lake.

"When I was a kid I would come over sometimes for the fun of helping to work his nets and listening to his tall stories," Tony said. "He had a plank pier and a small shed for storing gear on an inlet that's just ahead. It's the only other structure I can think of for miles around . . ."

They burst onto a small crescent of beach, too narrow to accommodate a house. All that remained of the dock were bits of rotted planking that clung to barnacled snags of pilings. Tacked together from pieces of scrap lumber and tin, the shed had fared little better. Its flat, sloping roof showed jagged breaks and the tin was cancerous with rust.

Diana rushed forward, but Tony was quicker. He was around the corner of the windowless shed, jolting to a halt at the opening where the slatted door had rotted off its hinges.

Diana banged against him, and there was Cloty, spotlighted by the sunlight pouring through a gap in the roof. She lay on her side, hands tied behind her, ankles trussed with a piece of frayed rope, a dirty red bandanna gagging her mouth. Her old-fashioned black dress looked as if she'd been dragged through a pig wallow; her face was powdered with dust and grime; her hair was in strings. But her eyes were as snappishly alive as ever, peremptorily ordering Tony and Diana to quit standing there gawking.

Tony and Diana rushed in, shoulders meeting in a small collision. They dropped to their knees on either side of Cloty, Diana reaching to the back of Cloty's neck to jerk the bandanna knot loose while Tony stripped the cords from her wrists and ankles.

Tony helped the old governess to a sitting position. Cloty looked at Diana's tear-filled eyes.

"Guess you'd get weepy over a homeless pup," Cloty snorted.

"C-can't help myself."

Tony was massaging Cloty's wrists where the imprint of her bonds showed. "Never mind that," Cloty said. "Just tell me if my feet are still there. My ankles are dead asleep."

"Still there," Diana said.

"Then help me up on them!"

On either side of Cloty, Tony and Diana lent support as Cloty got up and hobbled out of the shed.

"Where's that crazy old coot, Ozar Fant?" Cloty demanded.

"Swamp running," Tony said. "He gave me the slip."

"Too bad. I'd like to ask him—among other things—if he's also been eating that swill he gave to me!" Cloty pushed Diana and Tony aside, trying out her feet with short, hobbling steps.

"What happened, Cloty?" Diana asked.

Cloty winced as circulation returned to her arches, but she kept moving back and forth. "I decided to have a look at the chapel ruins before I hauled Constable Comage out," she said. "I wondered if the St. Joan could have been pushed over from outside."

"It could have," Diana said. "I checked out the same thing."

"I didn't quite have the chance," Cloty said. "I was barely past the mausoleum when it seemed that the tallest pine in the forest fell squarely on my head."

"Did you see who struck you?" Tony asked.

Cloty rolled a look at him, as if peering over her non-existent glasses. "I was instantly out of it, my boy—until I groaned awake here with Ozar Fant hunkered dolefully beside me, doctoring my head with cold compresses."

"Then he didn't hurt you," Diana said.

"Not unless it was him that gave me the poleaxe," Cloty said. "He brought me food and water and apologized each time he tied me up, which was everytime he left the shed."

Cloty gave her prison a hard glower. "His apologizes were scant comfort while I froze by night and baked by day. Wonder I didn't catch my death!"

Cloty moved her arms, linking Tony on one side of her and Diana on the other. "Bless you. Somehow I knew help would reach me. I told Fant so. I made life as hard as I could for him, when he would come and ungag me and offer me that leftover rabbit stew. I told him . . ."

She stopped, her eyes lifting to Tony's face. "I told him Tony Devereau would find me and make him dance on hot coals."

Out of all of them, Diana thought, Cloty pinned her faith on Tony . . . and I'm beginning to understand why.

"Not quite like the cavalry," Tony smiled. "I left my bugle at home. But we've a couple of horses close by. How about I plant you sidesaddle, mount up behind, and we canter victoriously home?"

"Just sneak me in," Cloty said. "I wouldn't have a hound dog see me looking like this, if I could help it."

Tony's quip about a victorious return did little to dispell the gravity the three shared during the ride home. Diana knew the unanswered questions that throbbed through all their minds.

By the time they reached the stables, Cloty was showing gray-faced signs of exhaustion from her ordeal. Food, rest, and her unflagging spirit would restore Cloty in a day or two, Diana knew, but right now she was using her last reserves to spurn Tony's suggestion that she be carried into the house.

"Under my own steam, Tony," Cloty insisted.

Adding insult to injured pride, Mrs. Lafarge saw them from her kitchen, denying Cloty's wish to slip in unnoticed.

Mrs. Lafarge appeared briefly on the patio, then vanished inside with a shout. She returned with Philip, Robin, and Huxley in her wake.

They all crowded around, smothering Cloty with questions and solicitude. Philip immediately took charge: "Robin, Mrs. Lafarge, help Cloty upstairs. Huxley, fetch Nurse Abernathy to Cloty's room. Hurry, all of you! I'll call the doctor."

Cloty's protests fell in non-listening ears. She was bundled inside, Philip bringing up the rear and pausing only long enough to say to Diana and Tony: "You can tell me about it later in detail. Right now, Cloty happens to be first-things-first."

"Sure, Philip," Tony agreed patiently, watching them all fade inside, out of sight.

They were near the pool, and Diana sank at one of the metal tables. Tony eased into the wrought-iron chair opposite her. He looked all about.

"Well, Diana. Just the two of us. Getting to be a sort of habit, from the hour you arrived here."

He picked up her hand where it lay on the table

225

top. It was small and a bit grimy against his palm. His fingers closed about hers and his eyes came up to her face.

"And how about you, Diana? You look bushed. When did you eat last?"

It took her a moment to switch her hard train of thought. "At breakfast."

"No wonder," he said. "It's getting on toward dinner time. I'll get you something."

He started to rise, but she wouldn't release his hand. "Wait, Tony. I've something on my mind besides food."

He sank down in his chair. "What is it, Diana?"

"I'm not certain . . . The pieces are there . . ."

Her eyes worried over the problem. "One thing I do know. The things we've learned about Ozar Fant point beyond him, to someone else."

Tony nodded slowly. "That's true. Would he shut you in the crypt and then let you out with a warning to leave Devereau House? Sounds more like he was trying to protect you."

"The same with Cloty," Diana said. "It's far-fetched to think that he'd attack her violently only to carry her off and try, in his dull-witted way, to take care of her later. I think Ozar Fant was acting in character all the time, attempting to keep anyone from getting hurt."

"Except Lucy," Tony said bitterly.

226

"He might have tried in that instance, too, and failed. Perhaps he didn't realize what was about to happen in the ruined chapel, or he might have arrived too late, after the St. Joan had fallen."

"But why?" Tony asked. "What has kept him skulking about in the role of protector?"

Diana drew a shaky breath. "I think his rescue of Cloty and me was incidental. I believe his main objective was to protect the person he loved devotedly for a lifetime. His fixed idea was to keep her from doing harm which in the end would work to her own destruction. He did everything possible in his limited way to nullify her acts and point the evidence away from her."

Tony's lips whitened. "You're talking about Prospera Clantell."

"Yes, I am," Diana asserted. She gulped a breath. Talking it out with Tony, the pieces were falling in place, shocking little explosions tearing through her mind.

She gripped the edge of the table, pressing against it. "Don't you see, Tony? It's the only pattern that fits Fant and his actions. He was doing everything for the sake of Prospera Clantell! Scuffing out the marks made by the pitchfork when it was thrown at me from the hayloft. Opening the crypt for me. Taking Cloty to a place of safety. He was buying time, Tony, for himself and Prospera Clantell. He must have tried to get her to leave this place before she was exposed and it was too late for her."

Tony's face was drawn; nerveless, yet masking screaming nerves. "Yes," he said, "in her madness, her desire for vengeance, Prospera Clantell would have a motive for destroying Lucy, for making the Devereaus suffer to the final taste of anguish. She tried once . . . to kill my father. In her paranoia, I'm sure she would like to destroy us all . . . But she's dead, Diana!"

"How do we know?"

"Fant told people in the village . . ." Tony trailed the words off. His mouth jerked with a jolt of understanding.

"Yes," he said through his teeth. "Fant's word is the only evidence. But in his diary, he said she was no longer in the madhouse. She is gone, he wrote."

"That's it, Tony! If she had died, it would have been an underscored entry in the diary, the most important of all. Fant would have detailed her death, the place of her burial."

Tony drew a gathering of perspiration from his chin with the palm of his hand. "So instead of dying, Prospera Clantell escaped . . . One day, an old and commonplace fixture, she had her chance and slipped away."

"And Fant," Diana said, "did the very thing that came to him naturally. It must have seemed incredibly clever to him. He told a tale of her death to keep anyone here from suspecting a truth about an old woman. She was no longer recognizable as the once-beautiful Prospera Clantell, but Fant was afraid of questions that might be raised. The lie about her death is completely understandable. It was the first thing he did to protect her, to buy time until he could prevail on her to go away from Acadia."

"But the administrator of the asylum . . ."

". . . Would have notified the authorities in the area to be on the lookout for her," Diana broke in. "She was an old, indigent nobody in a crowded and harassed public institution. Probably no one on the staff today can remember when she first arrived there. She became an empty bed for someone on the public waiting list, and a routine record in massed police files. It happens all the time, Tony. Even young criminals who escape public mental institutions are rarely returned— until they have committed another crime, are caught, and routinely identified."

"I can't deny the truth of that," Tony said. "But where is she? Where has she been hiding?"

"Under our noses!" Diana lurched to her feet. "Tony, did you hire a menial about the time Ozar Fant started skulking about?"

The breath kicked out of him. "Myree!"

"The little gray topknot," Diana said bitterly.

"The maker of beds, scrubber of pots. The wiry old cat with the strength of a devil!"

Tony's chair fell with a clatter as he rose and threw a look toward the kitchen and at the window-doors of the playroom.

"If she is Prospera Clantell it would explain everything," he ground out, "including Fant's role from start to finish."

"If she isn't Prospera Clantell," Diana said, "nothing will explain it all. Myree was actually pilfering my room when I caught her there, not bringing fresh towels. She wanted to know who this stranger was, her intentions and purposes. She was the one person who could have overheard Cloty and me talking about a fresh investigation of Lucy's accident. She alone knew that Philip and I made a spur of the moment decision to go riding.

"In the weird world behind her eyes, Myree-Prospera saw both Cloty and me as threats. She had time to slip out to the barn while Philip waited for me to change clothes. She tried to scare me off with the pitchfork, and later by locking me in the crypt. It was she who attacked Cloty—and Fant who undid part of her work through love and fear.

"She was the only person spooked by my appearance after I was locked in the mausoleum—not because I'd burst into the kitchen unexpectedly, but because I'd entered the house at all!"

Tony rounded the table, his eyes hard on the

house. "That's more than enough, Diana. The authorities can nail down any little details later. Right now, the thing is to find Myree . . . rather, the old hag that Prospera Clantell became. Keep a sharp eye on the grounds. I'll start a search of the house."

A flash of movement, he was inside almost before he got the words out.

Standing alone, Diana shivered. Her gaze swept the patio, the side yard, the gardens and stables. The scene was so peaceful it didn't seem real. Reality was Cloty and Lucy . . .

Diana's knuckles jerked up to her mouth.

Lucy!

And Philip, as they'd ushered Cloty inside, saying: "Bring Nurse Abernathy to Cloty's room . . ."

Dear God, Lucy was abandoned, utterly alone!

It was the chance for which Prospera Clantell would have watched and waited.

"Tony . . ." Diana said in a strangled voice.

She was rooted. Then she saw the playroom swirling toward her and knew that she had managed to move.

She rushed through the playroom, the dining room, into the great hall.

Silence. Emptiness. There was a metallic taste in her mouth, and she had the wild notion of a strange odor. Like death.

Half tripping and clutching the bannister in her

headlong rush, Diana fastened her eyes on the upper gallery.

She came up out of the stairwell gasping. The gallery was deserted, and without hesitating she ran on toward Lucy's room.

The door was closed. She turned the knob, threw it open, and strangled on a silent scream.

There was the gray old cat, an image of madness beside the bed, eyes and lips wet with gleeful satisfaction as she pressed the pillow tighter and tighter against Lucy's helpless face.

She was finishing the job she'd thought finished in the ruined chapel. It was all just and right in the warped darkness of her mind. It was judgment and execution. It was the taking of a Devereau child for the child of her own that a Devereau had taken . . .

"Myree!"

The withered old face had already lifted. She spun from the bed, cat quick, leaving the pillow over Lucy's face. Darting to the table where the sterilizer stood, she grabbed a pair of sharp scissors, and she came stalking.

"You!" she said. "I knew you for an enemy the minute you came. You and Lucy Devereau, peas in a pod . . . I should have thrown the pitchfork straighter!"

"Wait, Myree . . . Relax. Let me say something to you."

"Nothing to say. You're as bad as the Devereaus. You'll get what's coming!"

She circled, scissors lifted, backing Diana toward the wall.

"Lucy was first," Myree-Prospera mouthed the words. "Now you. After that, Tony. All the Devereaus—except Huxley. I want Huxley to live. To remember and be sad for all the things he said and did to me. Once he was powerless against the touch of my lips. I want him to suffer not one death, but a thousand times over, remembering how powerless he was against the work of my hands!"

Diana saw the attack spark in the sunken eyes. She ducked and reeled aside as the scissors flashed.

The weapon scarred the wall plaster. Myree fell back, spun, and bore in again.

Diana snatched the pillow from Lucy's face, swinging it up and around as a shield. She felt the impact, heard the quick tear of fabric, and saw Myree through the explosive shower of feathers.

She stumbled alongside the bed, drawing the old woman away from Lucy. Myree came on quick, padding feet, the scissors stabbing.

Diana threw the remnants of the pillow in Myree's face and grabbed the thin, tensile wrist. They staggered to the middle of the room, Myree's free hand clawing.

233

Then the old woman was suddenly torn away, and the room was filling with people. Tony in the lead, pinning Myree's arms to her sides. Philip, with Robin breathless beside him.

And Abernathy, rushing to Lucy, giving them a look over her green-starched shoulder.

"She's still breathing," Abernathy said, "and quite strongly."

"Are you sure?" Diana quavered.

"Of course I'm sure!" Then with a faint smile Abernathy added: "I'd stake my reputation as a first-class nurse on a favorable prognosis. You reached her in time, Diana."

Diana's head moved in a wordless thanks. She felt a little limp, realizing that Abernathy was bustling her, Tony, Philip, and Robin out of the room.

In the upper gallery, they were momentarily an uncertain group, dazed, and relieved.

Then Robin smiled with deadly sweetness. "You are our heroine, Diana. The way you tackled Myree . . .with the ferocity of a bayou wildcat. My dear, I'd lay odds you could fight the toughest New Orleans barmaid to a draw!"

Diana's response to the nasty remark was a single cool look, at Philip. His eyes flashed irritation for Robin—but he didn't seem able to disengage himself from Robin's possessive touch on his arm.

Diana turned away. Why hurt Philip by letting him see the reflection of pitying truth in her eyes? He was no longer the self-possessed stranger, but an image that had been put together out of borrowed habits, secondhand opinions and ideas, borrowed strength. He needed Robin. She was inevitable for him. Diana had thought once that Robin might twist and change him. And that was true. But he was waiting clay . . .

But Tony . . . her heart seemed to swell at the thought of his name. It had been Tony who'd rescued Cloty, overpowered Myree. Tony, like Lucy, always seeming somehow to meet the gritty situation. Tony with his moods to bedevil her—or raise her to the heights. Tony with that lurking inner strength to ask questions and admit uncertainties.

Yet all of that didn't matter. In this revealing second, a single thing counted. She was in love with Tony, just as he was, moods and all.

She was moving toward him now, content to have Robin hold Philip back with her little smug smile.

"Buy me a cup of coffee?" Diana asked.

"Sure," Tony said, taking her arm and guiding her down the stairway.

They entered the kitchen, and instead of bothering with coffee right away, Tony drew Diana to him.

"You aged me twenty years, you know," he said, "when I saw you fighting for your life with Myree."

His eyes imprinted every detail of her face, her lips, eyes, brow. He suddenly crushed her very

235

close, a rough sound in his throat. "I don't know the score on a lot of things," he breathed warmly against her hair. "But one thing I can be sure of for the rest of my life. I love you, Diana!"

The quiet conviction in his tone was a heady wine. She didn't trust herself to speak. She offered her lips in answer.

His kiss was a sweet fire, and when their lips had slowly parted, Diana laid her head against his chest.

She would be content to remain this way forever, she thought, just the two of them, insulated from the world and its conflicts. Problems such as Robin's greed to control Devereau sugar lands. Or was that a problem, really? Robin hadn't succeeded so far, and it might just be fun to watch Robin's frustration in the future.

"One more kiss and I'll make the coffee," Tony murmured. "You asked me to buy you a cup."

Diana lifted her face. "Did I?" she whispered.

Chapter 15

The following afternoon, Cloty, seated at Lucy's bedside, broke off reading a gossip item in the New Orleans paper when the door opened.

The intruder was Diana, and Cloty decided to grump only a little.

"Hi," Diana said to both Cloty and Lucy.

Lucy winked a reply, then mirrored a question.

"Yes," Diana nodded, "it's all over. Comage just called. They're taking Prospera back. Fant heard that she was in Comage's custody last night. The old man came in and gave himself up. I don't think they'll do much to him. Maybe a jail term to think over his dereliction in not revealing Prospera's whereabouts. After that, I guess he'll be free to toil out his pennies, buy his bus tickets, and journey upstate."

Cloty looked over the rims of her new spectacles as Tony strolled in.

"Abernathy," Cloty said, "aren't you getting a bit too lax?"

"Just for today," the nurse growled back from the refrigerator where she was arranging bottles of liquid diet.

Tony stood at Diana's side and put his arm about her shoulders. "Hi, sis," he said to Lucy. "Quite a girl we've got here, don't you think?"

Lucy blinked a yes.

"And some brother, I'd say." Diana slipped a glance at Tony's profile.

"We'll have the summer to show her what a brother," he said. "When autumn comes, we might even convince her that teaching in a bayou school is even more challenging than Kansas. After that . . . who knows?"

Yes, Lucy blinked. By all means, yes. We shall keep Diana with us forever.

Lucy underlined the meaning in her eyes with a small movement of her hand.

Her left hand.

The meaning of it struck Diana like a shower of sunbeams, a future of movement and life opening out for Lucy.

"Tony," Diana murmured.

"Yes?"

"Did you notice just now," Diana said in a quiet tone understating the beauty and magnitude of the

announcement, "that Lucy moved her hand? Not
her right hand. But her left."

It was like him to respond in an unlikely way.
His face mirrored no surprise.

"I have prayed that she would," he said.

If your dealer does not have any of the MAGNUM EASY EYE CLASSICS, send price of book plus 10 cents to cover postage to MAGNUM CLASSICS, 18 East 41st Street, Room 1501, New York, N.Y. 10017.